Tender
DANCE

Book 4 of the Lovers Dance Series

---

by Deanna Roy

Six-Time *USA Today* bestselling author of
The Forever Series
The Lovers Dance Series

Sign up to be notified about new releases via email or
text.

Casey Shay Press
PO Box 160116
Austin, TX 78716
www.caseyshaypress.com

E-ISBN: 9781938150685
Paperback ISBN: 9781938150678

Library of Congress Control Number: 2017905604
eBook version 3.0

Summary

Livia's tenuous relationship with her child is shattered. Lost and distraught, she returns to dance as her solace and lands a part in a major ballet. As both their careers ignite, the couple faces a difficult choice — follow their careers or stay with each other.

Get emails or texts from Deanna about her new releases:
Deanna's List

Chapter One

It's a long, long way down.

I wind my foot around the fluttering blue tail of silk. My hands grip the fabric like a lifeline. The highest cushioned mat is a solid ten-foot drop. If I miss it, it's another ten feet to the floor.

Blitz stands below, hands on his hips, looking up. He seems small, like an action figure rather than a man. His black hair shines and the sexy scruff on his face looks darker from up here.

Bex, our instructor, also watches me, her gaze occasionally shifting to the tall mats, as if she fears she might have to dash up the stairsteps of cushions to rescue me.

I'm attempting the biggest aerial silk drop I've ever done.

The other dancers in the gymnasium have paused

to watch. They've gotten used to us being here, and the novelty of two reality TV dance show stars in their workout space has worn off. But this is new. I'm at the tip-top of the silks, swaying near the swivel hook, and I've hung out there too long.

"Do the twist and the turn like we practiced," Bex calls up. "You're fine!"

Except I'm not fine. My arms are shaking even though I'm not putting any stress on them. I have a foot lock engaged, so it's like I'm standing on the ground.

As long as I can ignore that the ground is way, way down there.

Blitz and I have been working on this move for a couple months. We first learned it from our instructor in LA while we were still filming the last season of *Dance Blitz*. Then we picked it up again here, back in San Antonio. We don't plan to do any more television episodes, and aerial silk work is fairly impractical, mostly used by circuses and talent shows.

But we enjoy it.

Usually.

Currently, I'm not a fan.

"You've got this, Princess," Blitz calls up. He's deadly calm. He has total faith. There isn't so much as a hint of concern on his face.

Not that he's close enough that I could see it.

I close my eyes. I'm not sure what's really getting

me. We have practiced the parts of the drop closer to the ground a hundred times. It's just that to do the full extension of it, I have to be high. We had to pick a day where I did it all.

Today is the day.

And I'm feeling anxious.

"Let's take this one step at a time," Bex says. She's climbing the mat tower now so she can get closer. "Don't think about anything, just do what I tell you."

I open my eyes and watch her get closer. "Okay," I say.

"The triple turns will slow your descent," she says. "You just need to finish the wrap. Start with the left."

My right foot is the one in the lock, so it's not hard to go ahead and sweep my left leg around the loose silk.

"Good," Bex says. She's at the top of the mat now and reaches out for the black silk hanging next to my blue set. She pulls it toward her, then quickly climbs her way up to me. Now we're next to each other, as if we're having any common conversation.

"Release the foot lock." She holds herself up on the silks and wraps her left leg so that we are in the same position.

This is harder to do. As soon as I release the foot lock, I have to suspend myself.

"Release it," Bex says. Her voice is no-nonsense.

I let out a long rush of air and release the foot lock.

"There you go," Bex says. "Now engage the right leg in the wrap."

My arms continue to shake. I don't look down, though, not even to get another glimpse of Blitz. I wrap my leg and slide down into the splits.

"Now pull up the extra and wrap for the drop," Bex says.

I'm better now, all business, as I catch the tails of the silk and pull them up. I twist and turn the way I've practiced, making additional rolls to accommodate the extra height, and adding loops to allow for brief free falls.

"You've got it," Bex says. "Everything looks good."

She releases her own foot lock and slides down until she is level with the mat, then swings over. She lands lightly on its surface, taking the black silks with her to keep them out of my way.

"Check, catcher," she says.

"Check, catcher," Blitz says.

"Check, flier," she says.

"Check, flier." My voice sounds steadier than I feel.

Bex doesn't hesitate. "On three, two, one, GO."

I dive forward.

The key to aerial silk drops is in the preparation, the turns of the fabric around your body. Once you start the sequence, there isn't much to do other than let the pattern unfold and keep yourself centered and falling straight.

The air rushes by. My hair is tightly bound to avoid getting caught in the fabric on the way down. I feel an occasional lurch as one of the looser drops lets me fall for a second, then it catches again. I roll forward, the last silk tight around my waist, then I'm done with the silks and dropping.

Into Blitz's arms.

"Gotcha," he says.

The gym erupts in claps and cheers. Blitz turns around, keeping me tight against him, then rolls me over his back and I cartwheel out of the move to stand beside him.

More whistles and cheers. Bex rushes down the stairsteps of mats to reach us.

"You did it!" she says. "You're about to be as technical as I can take you. You only need to add some form to make the wrap look dance-like as you put it together."

Blitz bows theatrically. Jenica, who owns the studio, claps her hands together over her head. Once the applause dies out, everyone returns to their workouts.

That's one nice thing about Jenica's. Everyone is focused on their work. Nobody videos or does live feeds or tries to take pictures. They respect each other's practice time, even if a private image of me and Blitz would fetch a decent price in the tabloids and most everyone here could use the cash.

Blitz turns me in a circle. "That was the most amazing move that no one will ever see!" he says.

"There is bound to be an act somewhere that would love this," Bex says. "The name Blitz Craven draws a crowd."

Blitz picks up his towel and shakes his head. "That's okay. We are more than happy to step far away from the limelight." He takes my hand. "We're looking for a house. Working on our ballet. Taking it easy."

Bex nods. "I get that." She glances at her watch. "And, on that note, time for me to pick up my little guy."

"Thanks for getting us to this level," Blitz says. "See you next week."

"Sounds good. Schedule with Weeza!" Bex hurries toward the door, scooping up her bag from the cubbies on the way out.

"Ah, Weeza," Blitz says. "I don't think she'll ever love us."

"You can't win them all," I say.

Weeza works here as the scheduling manager, and she despises Blitz and his commercial dance. The more successful his TV show got, the more she would speak up with her disdain.

We walk through the gym, admiring the ballerinas at the barre and the ballroom couples in the far corner.

"It's not Dreamcatcher, but I like it here now that we've found the right instructor," Blitz comments as we slip on our shoes. We have to do our aerial work barefoot.

"There's definitely room for more than one studio for us," I say. "But Dreamcatcher will always be special." I learned ballet there, and it's where I met Blitz. I also teach a wheelchair ballerina class, which includes my four-year-old biological daughter Gabriella. She doesn't know I am her mother. No one knows except Blitz. Dancing there keeps her close.

It's why we're settling down in San Antonio instead of LA. Plus Blitz's parents live here.

My parents are in town as well, but even though almost six months have passed since I left home, they still won't talk to me. I've tried twice since the show ended to see them again. But unfortunately, they heard about some of the sexier clips, and my father said a "dirty whore" like me had no place in their family.

I don't know any way to fix that.

We've just collected our things when we spot Weeza blocking the door. She's in her usual outfit of slashed tights and plain black leotard, her short blond hair in little spiky pigtails all over her head.

"Weeza!" Blitz says. "Let me guess. You finally figured out that you can't live without me."

Weeza's expression is more self-satisfied than usual. She leans against the door frame and crosses her arms. "You're not going to be laughing when you check your phones," she says.

Blitz's smile doesn't falter. "I KNEW you were a secret fan," he says. "You've been following me all along."

"As if," she says. "Besides, it's not even about you this time." She angles her head at me. "It's about her."

Weeza's otherworldly green eyes, probably colored contacts, pierce mine. My heart hammers inside my chest. The press and social media mentions since the final episode of *Dance Blitz* a month ago have been more positive than not. Everyone felt our relationship was genuine and was glad for how the show ended.

Besides, the machine has already kicked in to promote the new bachelor for the show, Mack Williams. Within a few months, Blitz and I will be distant has-beens. Our only appearance will be on the final episode of the next season.

I don't know what anyone would say that would make Weeza come seek us out. But my heart is still a little accelerated from the intense aerial drop. So I'm probably a little edgier than usual as I tell her, "I'm used to it."

She shrugs. "It's none of my business. But if my ex's new girlfriend decided to fork over a story about my secret baby to the Internet, I'd be pretty dang mad."

My head whips around to Blitz. His eyebrows have hit his hairline.

"Show me," he demands.

Weeza turns her phone to him.

He takes it from her, swiping rapidly with his finger.

I can't look, imagining the worst, pictures of Gabriella next to mine. Her adopted mother's anger.

Never getting to see her again.

Blitz passes the phone back.

I manage to get out a few words. "How bad?"

He takes my arm. "They don't know who she is. Only that she exists." He nods at Weeza. "Thanks for the heads-up."

"My pleasure," she says with an attempt at sarcasm, but it doesn't have its usual bite.

My legs threaten to wobble out from under me as we head outside to my little white Volkswagen convertible. I finally got my driving permit, something my family hadn't allowed, and I have been working through my driving hours so I can take the test.

But I'm not up for that extra stress today. I pass the keys to Blitz and he gets behind the wheel.

When we're sealed up in the car, no one to overhear us, I ask him, "So what happened?"

Blitz starts the engine. "It wasn't Denham. It was some girl he was dating. They broke up and she decided to talk to the tabloids. She said you had his baby when you were teenagers. That you put the baby up for adoption and he never got to see her."

"Nothing else?"

"That's probably all she knew."

"Denham didn't talk?" My pulse flutters madly, as if my heart itself is trying to run away.

"Apparently he's back in jail."

I stare out the window. I had hoped somehow that he'd get his life back together after we bailed him out that last time.

But he told this woman our secret. And she'd seen an opportunity.

"Why does anyone believe her?" I ask.

"Because I bailed him out of jail and the attorney's agreement mentioned a kid. She has the paperwork."

"That handwritten thing he made in jail?"

"They have shots of it with the date. Everyone knows I was there that day."

Crap.

We drive along the bright streets, green and vivid for late spring. When my heart calms a bit, I pull out my phone. As long as they don't know who Gabriella is, it's still okay. They can say what they want about me or Denham.

I don't know what Blitz read or how much he saw, but I only have to look at a few headlines to see that he's wrong about how much has gotten out.

Yes, the girlfriend told everyone about the baby. And the adoption. But she also told one very telling detail. One that will sink us.

The secret baby is now in a wheelchair.

Chapter Two

"We have to talk to Danika," I tell Blitz. "Now."

Blitz turns abruptly, heading toward Dream-catcher rather than the place we've rented while we look for a house. "What's up?"

"One of the sites says she's in a wheelchair."

He slams his hand on the steering wheel. "I didn't catch that part."

"You were skimming." I feel like throwing up. It's Wednesday, and I just saw Gabriella yesterday for our wheelchair ballerina class. Tomorrow is our private lesson with her. I wonder if the other instructors are figuring things out. We've long suspected Danika, the owner of Dreamcatcher Dance Academy and a personal friend, has figured out that Gabriella might be mine.

"Can you see if she's there?" Blitz asks.

I nod and send a quick text to Danika that I'm headed her way.

I get a response almost immediately.

I guess you've seen the news. Come on over.

I tell her when we'll arrive and tuck the phone under my leg. I don't want to read any more gossip sites. I don't want to know what they are saying.

But the buzzes continue. I look, assuming it's Danika. But it's not.

It's my friend Mindy. She hasn't written me in almost four months, since her parents took away her phone. She's only sixteen, another homeschooled girl from my church. She's finally found a way to reach me.

I read the message greedily.

Livia, it's Mindy. This isn't my phone. I figured out how to text you from the church laptop. I got to watch your show at my grandma's house. She goes to bed early! You looked beautiful. But I saw the news today. How can they tell those lies about you?

I write her back.

Not lies. I did have a baby. The father is in jail. It was a long time ago and I never told anyone.

How old were you?

I hate this. I hate having to spill to anyone. And I hate that I never told her before.

Fifteen.

Yowsa, Liv! Where is she?

I glance over at Blitz. He's focused on the road, looking intense and angry.

Mindy is asking pretty private questions. And she has only rarely ever called me Liv.

What if this isn't really Mindy I am talking to? The number is unfamiliar. She said it was from a laptop. What if someone is pretending to be her?

"Do you remember my best friend's name?" I ask Blitz.

He frowns. "You were pretty tight with your assistant on the show, Jessie," he says.

"No, from before I left home."

His mouth pulls down again. "The one who got grounded from talking to you?"

"That one."

He bites his lip. "Mandy? Melanie?"

"Mindy," I say.

"Yes, Mindy. What about her?"

"She's writing me, or she says she is, from an unfamiliar number. She's asking questions about the baby, and now I'm worried it's not really her."

"Ask her something only she would know."

I nod. I ignore her question about Gabriella and text her again.

How is my brother Anthony doing?

After a moment, she replies.

Autocorrect? You mean Andy. He seems a little sad. I think he misses you.

Okay, so she knows my brother's name.

Did you have to put away the church decorations alone?

No, Irma helped. I think she misses you too.

Okay, it's her.

But she's dropped the question about the location of my daughter, and even if she is my friend, I don't know if I should answer it in writing. Instead, I ask her something else.

Can you meet at the park today?

Not sure. I can try.

I'll be there from 2 to 3 for the next three days.

I know this was a common "recess" time back when we were both homeschooling.

I will try. Gotta go before Irma gets back.

Thanks for finding a way to write me. I miss you.

Miss you too.

"It was her," I tell Blitz. "I'm going to try and meet her sometime over the next few days."

"Did she get her phone back?" he asks. He exits the highway. We're almost to Dreamcatcher.

"No, she wrote from the church laptop."

"When are you supposed to see her?"

"I told her I'd hang out at the park for an hour for the next few days."

"I'll pick up another phone. You can slip it to her and get back in contact."

I reach out and squeeze his arm. Blitz got a phone for me when we first knew each other. I had no other way to stay in touch with him. "That's a good idea. Thank you."

"I'll get Ted on it," he says. When we reach a red light, he sends a quick text.

"I'm glad you brought him on full-time as a bodyguard," I say.

"I'll miss Duke, but he is loving LA too much to leave," Blitz says. "Sounds like he and Mack are hitting it off."

In addition to taking over the show, Mack is renting out Blitz's old condo, which is full of reality show cameras. We are more than glad to be away from all that.

"Did Mindy see the news?" Blitz asks. "Is that why she wrote you?"

I nod. This is apparently too big for anyone to ignore, even homeschooled teenagers.

We approach the front of Dreamcatcher Dance Academy. My soul always feels calmer looking at the tall circular entrance. Bad things don't happen to me here. It's my special place. I have to believe this will be okay.

"Isn't that Gwen's SUV?" Blitz asks.

I scan the parking lot. "It looks like it." Now my pulse ratchets up again. This isn't a day for Gabriella to be here to dance. But Danika didn't mention

Gabriella's adopted mother Gwen being at the academy.

"Did you miss anything else in the links?" Blitz asks. "Are you sure they didn't find her already?"

"There were a thousand links," I say. "I just read the top ones."

"The celebrity sites will look for her," Blitz says.

And we both know the presence of Gwen at the academy doesn't bode well for keeping her hidden any longer.

All my secrets are about to be laid bare.

Chapter Three

❧

S uze looks up from the front desk as Blitz and I enter the building.

"Gwen and Danika are in the office," she says. "Gwen's pretty upset."

"Has she been here long?" I ask.

"Less than five minutes," she says.

I glance over at Blitz. He takes my hand and squeezes it. "Let's face this together," he says.

Tears prick my eyes. Gwen has figured it out. It makes sense that she would. She looks at my daughter every day and sees me twice a week. Once she knew I had a baby, she would recognize the resemblance. It's obvious to anyone who knows.

We cross the foyer and head through the doors to the side with the recital hall and Danika's office. My feet feel heavy. I just thought that a twenty-foot drop on an aerial silk was the scariest thing I would do today.

I am terrified.

Danika's door is closed, which is very rare. Her office is already isolated on the opposite side of the building from the dance classes. I knock on the solid wood surface.

No one calls out, but after a moment, Danika opens the door. She nods at me. "Hello, Livia," she says. She swings it wide. "Gwen is here."

My daughter's adopted mother has her head in her hands, her elbows braced on the edge of Danika's desk. She doesn't look at me as we all enter.

Blitz stands back in the corner. I take the chair next to Gwen. Danika settles back in her seat on the opposite side of the desk.

Danika speaks first. "Gwen wants to know if Gabriella is your daughter," she says. "She's the right age, and the resemblance is definitely there."

I glance over at Blitz. He nods. Gwen hasn't changed her position. All I can see is her curly dark brown hair and the curve of her back in a gray sweater.

"Yes," I say. "I gave birth to Gabriella on May 12, 2012. She was six pounds and eight ounces. Fifteen inches long. They tried not to let me see her, but I held her once for a few minutes before they took her away."

"At 8:52 p.m.," Gwen says. "We were downstairs."

"That's what they told me," I say. "The case-worker didn't want me to know if she was a boy or a girl. She was terrible. But I was so scared. I didn't say anything."

Gwen looks up and her eyes meet mine. She looks anguished. "The caseworker *was* awful," she says. "I never liked her, but she brought us our daughter." Her gaze drops. "That was the happiest day of my life."

"It was the worst day of mine," I say simply.

This makes her sit up straight. She looks back at Blitz, then to me. "You're going to take her, aren't you? You have money. Lawyers. You're trying to win her love with these dance lessons so you can have her." She stands up so abruptly that her chair falls back. "Don't you dare! Don't you come near her! Don't you ever look at her again!"

Danika also stands. "Gwen, I assure you, this will be okay."

Gwen turns on her. "What do you know? I've already lost my husband! I can't have children of my own! She will take the only thing that matters to me!" Gwen points at me, her finger an accusation.

"I wouldn't!" I try to say, but it comes out weak and dry.

Gwen stands and hurries for the door. "Don't talk to me!" she says. "I'm hiring a lawyer! Stay away!"

And she's gone.

Danika sinks back down in her chair. She doesn't speak for a moment.

Blitz comes up beside me and wraps his arms around my shoulders. "We have no intention of trying to take Gabriella," he says. "Livia means no harm."

"Harm has been done," Danika says. "Anyone here could connect the dots as well as Gwen has done." She presses the heel of her hand to her forehead. "I think it's best if the two of you take a leave from the academy."

When I make a small strangled sound, Danika looks up sympathetically. "I know it's hard, Livia. I have suspected Gabriella was yours for a while, since that boy came here shouting about your baby. I should have acted on it. I am equally to blame."

"We understand," Blitz says. "Please extend to Gwen, if you get a chance, our regret and that we have no intention of fighting the adoption."

"I'll never see her again," I choke out.

"You've put your name in her files," Blitz says. "She can find you when she is eighteen."

That's an eternity. She's only four. My body feels liquid, like my strength has left me. I want to go back in time. Never go on Blitz's show. Never be in the limelight. Never step from the quiet shadows. At least then I could see the little girl I had been forced to give up.

"Let's go," Blitz says. He tries to lift me from the chair, but I can't do it. I can't find any strength to move.

"I'll let you two have this space for a little while," Danika says. "I need to think about how to broach this topic with the staff and the other mothers in Gabriella's class. I would hate for them to reveal her identity to the gossip sites, either accidentally or on purpose."

I can't answer her. I thought I'd grown so strong in these past months by Blitz's side. But I'm overwhelmed again by shame. Not just in getting pregnant. But in finding my daughter, following her, inserting myself into her life.

I should have left them alone.

I did everything wrong.

I can't even cry. I'm so empty, so bereft of anything. Danika leaves the office, closing the door behind her.

"We'll get through this," Blitz says.

His words do not comfort me. "How?" I manage to say, words rising up from the vastness inside me, the huge empty hole.

"Because we have to," he says. "We can't let this swallow us up."

My vision is dark, as if the lights have gone out. No matter where I look, within or without, I see nothing but darkness anywhere.

I had one thing I held most dear, and I lost it.

Chapter Four

⁂

Over the next few days, the world tries to figure out where my baby could be. I guess because it is fun for them, they make all sorts of wild speculations, from the current Gerber baby to child stars on TV shows. Most of them conveniently leave out the fact that they know she's in a wheelchair as they post comparison pictures of me and all manner of kids.

They want someone adorable, already famous, a meaty bit of gossip. It's fine by me. This way they won't actually find her.

I don't go to the park to meet Mindy. I don't leave the house at all. Ted reports that everyone is trying to find us for interviews. We've gotten sympathetic messages from half the *Dance Blitz* cast. Even Mariah and Christy, two of the finalists from the show, have extended their support.

On Friday, Blitz sends Ted to hang out at the park with a phone for Mindy, but she doesn't come. I figure she already went there and gave up. I know it had to be hard for her to try it. Her parents are just as protective as mine were.

I've blown that too.

But on Sunday afternoon, four days after everything blew up, I get the surprise of my life. Mindy texts me.

I love my new phone! Thank you! I'll hide it forever and ever! Mindy.

I look up at Blitz, who sits on the floor by the sofa that has been my semipermanent home since the meeting with Gwen.

"I made Ted go to church this morning," he says. "He spotted Mindy and was able to pass the phone to her."

A tear squeezes out of my eye. "Thank you," I say. I send a quick text to Mindy, then set the phone down again.

"You going to see her?" Blitz asks. I know he is concerned. I haven't gone anywhere or worked out or danced since Wednesday.

"Maybe soon," I say. I don't know what else to tell him. That everything seems pointless now? That nothing he does will really help?

I want to pull myself together. I have him. I have Mindy back, thanks to him. I have money, a career, a home. I have dance.

But letting Gabriella go this second time is worse than the first. I could have prevented it. I didn't put her first. I let myself be vulnerable. I exposed her.

Blitz slides me forward on the wide cushions and fits himself behind me. He curls around my body, strong, stalwart, caring.

I just don't know what to tell him that will help.

I SHOULD HAVE KNOWN BLITZ WOULD HAVE MORE ideas.

Mindy is taking horse-riding lessons, I learn, and once a month the group joins a trail ride around a property on the outskirts of San Antonio.

Blitz immediately signs me up for the ride despite my objections that I've never ridden a horse in my life. He proclaims me terribly un-Texan and assures me that tenderfoots like myself get horses that don't need any guidance or direction. They just follow the pack.

When we arrive at the barn, Mindy is still with her mother, so Blitz and I hang out in the car until she is alone. She's turned seventeen in the months I haven't seen her. She's tall and lovely, her brown hair in twin braids that reach past her shoulders.

Her jeans are loose, and she wears a plain yellow T-shirt. She's like a bit of sunshine from my dark past.

As soon as I'm out of the car, Mindy spots me and runs to me like we're long-lost lovers in a meadow.

Her slender arms come around my neck and I've forgotten what it's like to have a friend of my own, away from Hollywood and television, all those people who might have an agenda or a motive for seeking me out.

"You look so different!" she exclaims, touching my hair. "You're so grown up!" She glances at Blitz and leans in close to my ear. "So what is the answer to our good-in-bed question?"

I laugh, and the sound is so foreign that I'm almost startled by it. I haven't heard it since the news of Gabriella got out.

"I'll have to tell you later," I whisper.

Blitz's grin is wide as he waves us off. "You girls have fun. Don't run off with any cowboys."

Mindy watches him get back in the plain gray car that we drive around when we don't want to attract attention. "You gotta tell me everything," she says. "I've missed it all since you left for LA."

"This better be a long ride," I say. "Because there's a lot to tell."

The day is outrageously hot and the horses plod along a trail that shimmers in the heat. There are about a dozen of us, led by a tough-talking sun-weathered lady in a worn cowboy hat.

The first few riders are young boys, maybe ten years old, then a newlywed couple, then three accountants in town for a convention. Mindy and I are last, followed by a handsome twenty-year-old, who was introduced as the son of one of the owners of the horse barn.

Mindy keeps looking behind us, torn between our secret conversation and keeping his attention.

"My parents would never have let me do a ride like this," I say. "Not this close to a real live man."

Mindy glances back again, notices the man is watching her, and blushes for the thousandth time. "I think mine figured not much could happen on the back of a horse."

"What have they said to my parents?"

"Not much. Mine expressed their concern that yours wouldn't talk to you. Your dad called you a —" she stops abruptly. "He said some unkind things that made my mom decide to speak to them less. They haven't done anything together since you left. Poor Owen misses your brother Andy. He was his only real friend."

"It's my dad," I say. "And I know exactly what he said. He said it to my face."

We round a small hill that looks down on a shallow valley. It's pretty, although sparse and dry. A brutal Texas summer is coming.

"You have to tell me all about Hollywood," Mindy says. "What was it like being on TV? Do reporters follow you everywhere? What is Blitz really like?"

I smile at her. "Hollywood is a business," I say. "It's hard to make real friends. You have to realize everyone is there to cut a deal." My horse whinnies, the first attitude she's shown since we started, and I grip the reins.

Mindy and I look at her like she might take off, but she settles back in the leisurely pace in our line of horses.

"Just joining your conversation," the cowboy behind us says.

Mindy flashes him a bright smile. "Thanks."

We realize he can probably hear us.

"You don't have to talk about it now," Mindy says.

"Oh, most things are stuff everybody knows," I tell her. "The cameras aren't always there. They can be an annoyance, but you learn how to rent cars or use back exits, or have your driver scout ahead before you go somewhere. We had plenty of time without worrying about them."

"It sounds so glamorous," Mindy says with a sigh. "Do you think you and Blitz will get married?"

I gaze out over the brushy landscape. "We haven't

33

really talked about it. Things are good. I got some money from the show too, so I could be on my own."

"Will you go to college now? I have to take my first SAT this summer," Mindy says. "Mom wants me to practice as a junior to help my score next year."

"Probably," I say. "I'll have to retake the test, I guess. I never saw my scores."

"Oh, there's a website. Just log in and put in your information. If you can prove your identity, they'll send them to you."

"Really?"

"Yeah. I read all about it. There's tons of kids out there who have problem parents. Once you're eighteen, your information is really yours."

"Blitz got me a car," I say. "I've been driving."

"Finally!" Mindy says. "Dad says maybe when I'm eighteen."

The woman at the front lets out a long singsong call. Her horse turns off the trail toward a shallow pond. They trot up to the water's edge.

The man behind us says, "We're going to take a little break here."

Our horses more or less follow the others to the water. Due to a cluster of trees, Mindy and I wind up a few yards down from the others. The cowboy follows us. "You girls need any help dismounting?" he asks.

I shake my head, lifting my leg up and around and hopping down.

"I think I might," Mindy says shyly.

I shade my eyes from the glare of the sun as the man leaps from his horse with practiced ease and approaches Mindy.

"Just lean my way," he says.

She lets go of the reins and falls sideways, right into his arms. I pinch my lips to suppress my smile. That girl is ready for a boyfriend, no doubt about it.

"You take lessons out here?" he asks her, setting her feet on the ground.

"Every Thursday," she says.

"That's my day off." He frowns.

"I could try to switch it," she says.

He grins at that. "You take them with Mary?" He walks forward to grab the reins of both horses and leads them closer to the others. My wayward mare resists. She only wants the water. She's not interested in true love.

"With Trish, actually," Mindy says.

"Trish does Monday and Friday too. We could see if she has openings."

"Let's do that," she says.

He looks at her a moment, then says, "I gotta check on all the mounts." He walks backwards, toward the others, still looking at her.

"All right," she says.

I realize the lovestruck kids are forgetting the basics. "Thanks for helping," I say to the man. "What was your name?"

He tips his hat back a bit, and I can see his blue eyes. Mindy's going to have it bad for this one. "Preston," he says. Then back to Mindy. "I'm Preston."

"I'm Mindy."

He lifts his hat and tips it forward in acknowledgment, and I have to bite back another smile. They are adorable.

"See you 'round, Mindy."

He walks toward the woman who leads the ride, glancing back every three steps.

When he's far enough away, Mindy squeals, "Oh my God, did you see those eyes?"

"I did!"

"I have to do another one of these. Have to. Have to." She moves close to her horse so she can peek around without being obvious.

Although, of course, she's obvious.

"You think you can get your lessons switched?" I ask her.

"I have to!"

Preston moves out of sight and she plops down in the soft grass on the bank of the pond. "I feel like singing or something."

This makes me laugh. "It does that."

"Is this how you felt? When you met Blitz? Like singing?"

I think back to that day in the studio at Dreamcatcher Academy, when I discovered Blitz watching me dance.

"No, I felt like dancing," I say.

"That makes sense," she says. "I'm like a water fountain bubbling over."

I sit down beside her. I can still recapture that feeling I had then, sneaking around, seeing Blitz when I could. This would be Mindy's obsession, like mine once was.

And I still have that. Blitz is with me through all this, getting my friend a phone, organizing time for us to be together. I have lost a lot. Gabriella. My family. My ballet teacher. Dreamcatcher Academy.

But not everything. I still have Blitz. And I have dance.

Chapter Five

The day after the trail ride, I hurt like I have never hurt before. Ten hours of dance? Nothing compared to the pain in my thighs and legs.

Blitz knew it was coming and booked a massage appointment for late the next morning.

As the woman sets up her massage table in the living room, Blitz sprawls on the sofa, biting into a bright red apple. "Probably I should have a stiff drink while this goes on, but I'll be healthy instead," he says.

The lady passes me a white robe to change into. "Why would you need a stiff drink for this?" I ask him.

But a few minutes later, I get it. The woman peels the white robe down and slides warm oil over my back. It's impossible not to groan with the pleasure of it.

Blitz pads off to the kitchen and I can hear the clink of bottles. This makes me smile. Not even noon.

When he comes back, he has a short glass filled with ice and probably bourbon. It's rare to see him with a drink. He kicks back on the sofa again.

The woman works her way to my legs. My groans become gasps as she hits the tough spots. "They really got your legs and glutes," she says. She shifts the towel high on my thighs.

Blitz coughs into his glass. I watch him quietly, trying to manage the initial discomfort of her working on the pained muscles. I feel air hit my backside and realize I'm pretty much naked on this table for him.

His eyes don't leave my body, sliding down and back up to meet my gaze. When the masseuse is faced away from him, he gestures to his crotch. I have to smile at the outrageous tent in his shiny workout shorts. I'm not sure who this massage is really for, him or me.

Gradually, the pain starts to work out of my muscles, and I can feel myself melting into the table. The woman's strong hands move up and down my legs to ankles to feet. I didn't realize how much strain

I'd put on the stirrups until she pressed into the arch of my foot.

"Really got you here too," she says.

I nod. But once again, the soreness gradually shifts into utter relaxation. I groan again, and ice tinkles as Blitz takes another drink.

The woman slides the towel over me. "Roll over," she says.

Blitz watches quietly as I turn onto my back. The woman moves my leg to work on the thigh, and the shift of the towel makes him cover his eyes.

This time a laugh escapes me. Poor tortured Blitz. I want to reach out for him now, send this woman away.

But there's something in the anticipation, the tension of the wait. I adjust a little and the towel slips down, exposing a breast. When Blitz looks again, his head drops back, eyes on the ceiling. He shakes his head like there's no way he can make it.

I close my eyes, reveling in how the pain yields to this woman's work. She heads back to my ankles, moving my foot in circles. I should do this more often.

When I look at Blitz again, he has covered his face with his forearm. The drink dangles from his other hand, near the floor.

"Would you like to extend the massage?" the woman asks.

Blitz and I answer simultaneously, "No!"

I smile at her. "I mean, that was wonderful. I think it's time for a nap now."

The woman nods and helps me sit up. I hold the towel to me, for her sake, even though Blitz keeps making motions with his eyes for me to drop it.

I shake my head, a smile on my lips.

I change into a light sundress while she packs her things.

The front door has barely closed when Blitz comes up behind me and reaches for the hem of the dress. "I don't think so," he says as he lifts it up and over my head.

"What if she comes back for something?!" I exclaim as he tosses the dress aside. I'm not wearing anything beneath it.

"Then she'll see you naked," he says. His hands are all over me, running along the places the massage had been. "I seriously could not wait one more second."

Blitz pulls me to him, his lips crushing against mine. My body glides along his in the shiny workout clothes, slippery still with the absorbed oils.

He lifts me up and wraps my legs around his waist. I can feel him through the shorts. His mouth is feverish and demanding as we walk through the house to the bedroom.

Each step causes me to slide against the length of

him, building a need in me that makes me impatient to arrive. We make it to the bed and he leans forward, dropping me onto the mattress.

The smooth comforter is cool against my back. Blitz steps aside and tugs at the curtains that cover a set of French doors leading out onto a small patio.

Light floods into the room from the backyard.

"I want to see every delectable inch of you," he says.

"You've already seen every inch of me."

"Not enough," he says.

He swiftly gets rid of his shirt and shorts. The sun wraps around his golden skin, each muscle defined, lighting up his dark hair. He is glorious, maybe even more now than when I met him. The aerial silk work has forced him to become stronger. His shoulders are broader, the sides of his chest more built out than before.

He places a knee on the bed and I reach out to slip my fingers along the shadows and planes of his body. He lets out a groan and leans over me, dropping another kiss on my mouth.

We connect only there until his hand reaches for me, starting at the curve of my waist and gliding up. His hand encircles a breast, his thumb crossing the nipple.

I sigh against his mouth. Being with Blitz never gets old. He is patient. He pays attention.

When my hips shift toward him, his hand starts its journey down. He pauses to circle a pattern around my belly button, making my body lift again, coaxing him to make his way to where I want him.

He smiles against my mouth. "Impatient, Princess?" he says. "I had to wait through an entire massage."

Instead of moving on down, his hand goes to my hip. "I should make sure she did a thorough job on these muscles." His fingers shift down my thigh, squeezing the muscle lightly. "Seems nice and relaxed. Does it hurt?"

"I don't know," I say, my voice strained.

"Mmm, I should keep checking." His hand shifts to the other thigh.

His face gravitates toward my breast, taking a nipple in his mouth.

I lift up again, feeling hot, and wet, and full of need. "Blitz," I say, almost a gasp.

"Mmm-hmm, I hear you," he says against my skin. His mouth moves over to the second breast, and I shift again.

His hand reaches way down for my shin, massaging my calf. I grasp his head, hanging on to his thick hair. If his hands won't obey, maybe I can convince his mouth to go where I want.

I push.

I feel his smile against me as he moves down, spreading hot kisses along my belly.

Then he's there, no more coyness, his hands spreading me wide, mouth delving into the folds. When his tongue hits my clit, I cry out in exultation and relief.

He wastes no time now, adding fingers, slipping them deeply inside.

My body responds, caught in the intensity, the pleasure already flooding my veins. Then he gets me there, over the brink, and I'm calling his name, shuddering and pulsating as the orgasm takes over everything else.

I'm gasping, barely functional, when he grasps my waist and flips me over. My hair is everywhere, escaping the loose knot from the massage, as he pushes me to my hands and knees and falls in place behind me.

"Not going to wait another minute," he says, his voice low.

His hands hold my hips as he slides inside in one smooth stroke.

I cry out again, my head down, pressing back into him.

His moves are powerful, like a jungle cat. Each stroke hits new territory, different from what he was pleasuring just a moment ago. My muscles clamp down, eager to move with him, take what he's offering, and make it work for him.

I lift higher and push back harder. Blitz moves faster behind me, his handhold tight and firm. It's quick-paced and hard, pounding against my body mercilessly, creating a drumbeat inside me.

"Jesus, Livia," Blitz says, his hands everywhere now, my back, my breasts, down across my belly. His fingers caress me again, and I want to weep, so many sensations, hard and soft, fast and long.

Then he slows down, each stroke luxurious and slow. I can't take it. I want more. I need him. Need it now.

But he takes his time, bringing me higher, making me wait for it, until I'm an archer's bow, stretched as far as I can go.

When he grasps my hips this time, one hand between my spread thighs, there is no stopping what's coming. His powerful thrust into me sets off the lightning storm of reaction. I'm gasping, crying, shaking with the intensity of this orgasm. I feel him flooding me, holding still, his hand on my back.

I drop my head to the bed, holding myself together by a mere thread. It's so often this way with Blitz. His desire, his care, his power. They all come together to reach parts of me I still try to hold inside. It's his love. It's mine. My losses. My baby girl. The dance.

I can't contain it all and have to let it spill out. Hot tears come down my face.

Blitz knows me. He understands the places I go. He smooths my hair away from my face and wraps his arms around me.

We shift sideways on the bed and he curls me up inside the protective shell of his body. I'm surrounded by him, his skin, his comfort, his love.

I'm going to move through this. I couldn't do it alone. But I don't have to. I have Blitz.

Chapter Six

Having Mindy back is a big part of my recovery from losing contact with my daughter. I follow the progression of her conversations with her cowboy Preston through her failure to move her lessons to his inability to change his schedule. She asks for another trail ride, and her father says no.

I remember those frustrating days, being unable to do anything for myself, always at the mercy of my parents.

I pass my driving test and get my license. There's a bit of a disaster at the DMV when Blitz and I are spotted and we end up getting escorted out of the public area due to our presence creating a "public disturbance." At least I get a private test with no wait.

But for days after that incident, I hear the ringing

shouts of people asking, "Where is your secret baby, Livia? Are you going to get her back? How could you abandon her?"

It's doubly hard because I don't get to see her on her birthday. It was the first one I would get to spend with her, as she started the ballet class a couple months after it passed last year. Just like with her first four birthdays, she turns five without me.

I spend the day at the condo, listening to *The Nutcracker* and watching the dance video the girls did with Blitz when I first met him.

Blitz has flowers delivered at 8:52 p.m., the moment she was born five years before. It's pretty much the sweetest gesture anyone has ever done.

I know I have to pull myself out of this. I just have to find a way.

With my ability to drive, I start volunteering at the church again. Irma, the church secretary, agrees not to mention it to my parents, on the basis that she wouldn't call the parents of any other adult member of the congregation. She still gets upset when she remembers how my father almost struck me the day I came for the adoption paperwork.

Mindy and I enjoy our time up there, filing things and gossiping and making plans for next year when she is eighteen too. Her relationship with her parents isn't nearly as troublesome as mine was, and I tell her to think about just coming clean about the cowboy and asking if she can go on dates.

Irma doesn't follow celebrity gossip, even mine, and hasn't realized that there is a public frenzy surrounding my daughter's adoption. When I tell her, we relocate the files to a safety deposit box the church owns, just in case.

I wonder how Gabriella is doing, if she misses us. I doubt Gwen told her about me. She has completely sealed up her Facebook page and I can no longer see anything about my daughter.

"You want to go over to Jenica's and dance?" Blitz asks. "It always helps."

I reluctantly agree. I really just want to collapse on the sofa again. But I can't do that.

I get myself up and pack my ballet things. Dance is always the solution.

When we arrive at the gym, Weeza doesn't make any rude remarks as we pass. I guess even she knows when to quit.

Inside, the aerial silks are down and the tall mats pushed aside. A huge line of at least twenty ballerinas fill the entire length of the barre.

We set our bags in a cubby and approach Jenica, who is presiding over the lesson led by Ingrid, who coaches most of the ballet students. The two could not look more opposite, with Jenica loose-haired in her usual bright jewel-toned leotard and scarf skirt, while Ingrid wears traditional pale pink and a tight ballet bun.

"What's this?" Blitz asks. "Invasion of the tutus?"

Jenica laughs. "One of the most famous Russian ballerinas has defected from her country and is putting together a tour here in the US. She needs an entirely new corps of ballerinas, principals, soloists, and chorus dancers, to back her. Male and female. She's holding auditions right here at the Dancery."

"Wow." Blitz turns to me. "You going to audition, Livia?"

I shake my head. There's no way I could keep up with a traditional ballet schedule. I have only been *en pointe* for six months. While I trained hard during the show, I spent a lot of time doing other types of dance. And with the Gabriella issue, I haven't worked out in almost two weeks.

Jenica looks me over. "Are you sure? You looked quite good on Blitz's show. You should throw your hat in the ring. Your celebrity could benefit you, as ticket sales are always a factor."

I don't bother to argue with either of them. I'm not really myself, low energy, depressed. The last thing I want to do is tour with a Russian ballerina.

But I did come here to dance. So when Jenica takes Blitz over to the trampolines to work on flips, I slip on my toe shoes and get in line with the ballerinas who are moving through the standard ballet poses with Ingrid.

I'm a little rusty, but after a half hour, I fall into the rhythm with the others. It's nice to turn off my brain and just move, toe out, *plié*, *relevé*, first position, step-step-leap.

Other ballerinas join us as the time passes, but no one leaves. The other girls are focused and determined, showing no signs of fatigue. I've heard a touring ballerina's day can last ten hours or more, so it makes sense that they would push themselves.

I watch Blitz when I'm angled the right way. He's working with two of the acrobats who often perform stunts on the triple trampolines. I keep my pattern with the girls, second position, third position, hold-two-three-four.

Weariness begins to set in, but I keep going. At one point, a man who looks very out of place strolls through the gym.

He's trying to fit in with jazz tights and a dance shirt. But the cut is wrong, same as his hair and the style of his short round beard. He's not from here, or anywhere I've been. His skin is pale, his eyes translucent. He misses nothing as his gaze runs down the line of ballerinas, pausing on a few.

He sees me, but I don't impress him much, and his attention focuses elsewhere.

This is enough to make me want to stop. I finish the eight-count, then step away from the barre.

Blitz notices when I break ranks and hops off the trampoline to head my way.

"That was quite a workout you did!" he says.

He seems pleased. We head toward the cubbies for our bags, and I pull out a towel to smooth the hot sticky strands of hair at the back of my neck.

The man notices Blitz and stops walking, his eyes wide. Then he looks at me again, his gaze falling to my ballet shoes. He's recognized us, and he's not as nonchalant about it as the others.

He takes out a phone, and I groan. He's going to Tweet or Facebook or otherwise disclose our location.

"Come on," I tell Blitz. "Before that guy tells the world where we are and we lose another secret dance spot."

Blitz turns to look at who I'm talking about. "Oh, that's Dmitri, the casting supervisor for that Russian dancer. Jenica said he might stop by. He's been pre-scouting the ballerinas."

"I thought they were doing auditions," I say.

"They are, but still, he comes. He wants to see their work ethic."

I'm sure he thinks mine is trash, but that doesn't bother me.

"I'm sure me quitting makes them look good."

Blitz waves to the other acrobats and takes my hand. "Anybody who knows who you are will recognize you have what it takes to perform. Being on a show like we were is grueling."

"It was." Ten weeks of twelve-hour days. I remember them well.

We cross the empty foyer. Weeza isn't there to torment us.

"You going to chauffeur me home, licensed driver?" he asks.

"Sure," I say. The more I drive, the better I'll feel about it. The producers are already making noise about Blitz coming up to do some clips for the next season of the show, and I want to be able to stay home and drive myself if I want to. Maybe I can even sneak Mindy away to see her cowboy.

I had plenty of people help me when I decided I wanted Blitz. Danika and the instructors at Dreamcatcher. Bennett and his wife Juliet.

Time to return the favor. Helping Mindy will definitely help me too.

Chapter Seven

The official appointment with the real estate agent arrives, and I vow to be involved and optimistic. We start out in the sunny kitchen of our rented house, reviewing the properties on the laptop so we can prioritize which ones we want to visit in person.

Annabella is the total opposite of the coiffed celebrity agent we had in LA. She's mid-sixties, wears jeans and an off-the-shoulder peasant blouse, and keeps her hair in a braid down her back. She's a friend of Lita's, who owns the restaurant Blitz and I went to on our first date.

She frequently lapses into bursts of Spanish, mostly expressions I have learned to interpret, some as inexplicable as "I'm going to throw my flip-flop at her." She calls all girls "Mama," even toddlers.

I like her fine. She's practical and if she sees us looking at a house that's "too big or too stupid," she whips the screen around and clicks to the next listing.

I want to feel something for the glamorous homes that flash across the pages, but it's not happening. It's one set of doors and lawns and rooms, then another. I pause on a limestone one with pale yellow trim, and Annabella immediately says, "That's the one I picked."

We agree to drive over and see it. It's in Alamo Heights, not far from Blitz's parents. Annabella sticks us in the back of her banged-up Prius. She's chatty on the way over, pointing out *taquerias* that have the best guacamole and other little hole-in-the-wall businesses I would never have noticed otherwise.

When we pull up to the house, I really hope that it will feel right, the way our house in LA did. I want to picture myself living there with Blitz, making breakfast, installing a barre in a spare room, sitting on the back porch.

But it's like there's a gray mist between me and everything else. No color can get in. Instead I think of Gabriella, and how she couldn't roll up those steps without a ramp. And I imagine a birthday party with girls in tutus and ribbon sticks. Something that can never happen.

It takes tremendous effort to open the door and get out of the car. Blitz is animated, commenting on the towering oak trees and a magnolia in the front corner. He points out the explosion of pink flowers by the walkway and the cute Adirondack chairs on the porch.

But all I see is what isn't there. What can't be there. I follow them up the stone path and step onto the porch. Annabella fumbles around with the key and gets the door open.

The foyer is bright and white, a curved set of stairs heading up to a landing. Above us are tall windows, and a chandelier dangles from the second floor.

"Perfect spot for a really big Christmas tree," Annabella says.

"It's May," I say with more edge to my voice than I intend.

Both Blitz and Annabella turn to me. Annabella glances at Blitz, and I can tell what she's thinking. *What are you doing with this Negative Nelly?*

"You okay, Princess?" Blitz asks.

This grates on me today. I'm not a child. *Princess* makes me think of the little girls, rolling around the ballet room, holding their light-up sticks like scepters.

"Will you ever stop calling me that?" I ask.

Annabella glances between us. "I'm going to check on the other rooms while you two settle in," she says and not-so-subtly escapes the tension.

Blitz folds his arms around me, pulling me close. "I thought you wanted a house. We don't have to do this now if you're not ready."

I lean my forehead against his chest. I want to feel normal. But there is this vise around my heart, and it's got a hold on me.

"Let's just walk around," Blitz says. "We'll pretend we're Weeza and talk trash about every room."

This does get a small smile out of me. We head off to the left, which puts us in a bright room with hardwood floors and a china cabinet built into the wall.

"See, this is where people stuff their faces," Blitz says in his best Weeza voice. "It's so stupid. Why does anyone need a room just to eat? In fact, eating is stupid."

We walk into a stubby hall with a pantry on one side and a sink and glass cabinet on the other.

"Why is there a sink here when there's a perfectly good one in the kitchen?" Blitz asks. "Totally ridic."

Another smile. We pass through a breakfast nook with a big bay window, then into the gleaming kitchen. Everything is new and updated.

I start to feel a little better about the house.

Blitz points to the oversized stainless steel refrigerator. "And water coming out of the fridge too? Waste. Of. Space."

Annabella pops her head through the archway on the opposite end. "Love the kitchen, right?"

"It's nice," I say, running my hands across the stone countertop. I imagine my mom cutting potatoes on her chopping board. Would my parents ever see my house? Probably not. Dad believes I am a whore.

Maybe I am. What does it matter? It's just a word. He is no saint himself.

But now I'm all knotted up again.

"Take a look at the fireplace in the family room," Annabella says.

My heart pings at the word *family*. I'm not really in one right now, am I? My parents don't speak to me. I can't see my brother.

Does Blitz count? He is a boyfriend, definitely. We've been together six months now. He seems happy, grinning at me as he takes my hand so we can go look at the fireplace.

The room is grand, cavernous, one wall made of stone, another floor-to-ceiling bookshelves.

The fireplace matches the stone wall, big chunks of limestone, a mantel built in.

Annabella holds out her hands. "I can see so many happy memories taking place in here."

I want to see the good things. To picture myself with Blitz.

But I can't help but see what won't be here. My brother Andy won't run race cars across the floor. My dad won't put his feet up and watch a football game with Blitz, even though he used to do just that with his own friends before everything went sour.

And Gabriella. She won't roll across the smooth hardwood. I won't sit on the sofa and work on her recital costume, taking up the straps or gluing on extra stars.

I turn to the French doors that lead to the backyard. It's all just pointless. "I don't want it," I say to Blitz. "It's not right."

He turns from the fireplace. "Okay, Livia. We definitely want it to be just right." He turns to Annabella. "Did we have a second choice to view?"

"Sure," she says. "Let me pull up another address."

"No," I interrupt. "No more today."

Blitz comes up and puts his arm around me. "You okay, Princess?"

"Please stop calling me that!" I say. "Please." The only princess is the one I can't see anymore.

Blitz lets out a long gust of air. "Okay, Livia." He looks over at Annabella. "Let's try this again another day. I'm sorry."

Annabella holds up her hands. "I get it. Big decision." She leads us to the front door.

I want to feel bad, but I can't. As I look back at the house that is probably perfect, I can't see anything good about it, only the what-ifs and never-wills.

Chapter Eight

I know I have to pull myself together. I know it.

Blitz is asked to do a talk show in New York and I send him on without me. I spend more time up at the church doing menial tasks and hanging out with Mindy and Irma.

We unpack every ornate cloth that has ever been used on the altar and start cleaning each one by hand. We want to preserve the hand-stitched crosses and other appliqués, many of them decades old.

Taking a soft damp cloth to the lovely linen is a balm for me. It's a simple goal, to make something beautiful again. I'm surrounded by the places that I once knew. It helps.

Irma pokes her head into the small sacristy to see how it's coming. She wears her favorite plum paisley dress and her brown hair is in its usual sloppy topknot. When she sees me, she approaches the sink to hold up a corner of the cloth I'm working on.

"I sure wish our predecessors had taken better care of these," she says.

"I'll get them in shape," I tell her.

She nods and lays the cloth carefully back down. "I wanted you to know Father Stephen will be here in about half an hour. I sense you've been avoiding seeing him."

I continue to sweep the gentle cleanser across a particularly stubborn pale brown stain on the linen. "He'll tell my parents I've been here."

"And he will protect your right to be here. He will not turn away a child of God from the Lord's house."

"I know. I just feel happy here. I've lost a lot lately, and getting this back has been helpful."

Irma pats my shoulder. "I know, child. And I can't abide by the way your father has treated you. But one day, you will have to mend that relationship."

"I don't see how," I say. "He only sees me the way he wants to."

"Perhaps Father Stephen can help him find forgiveness in his heart."

My pulse rockets. I want to tell her that I don't need forgiveness. That he is the one that needs it. But that's not very godly, so I bite back the words.

I keep my measured, easy pace on the altar cloth, and finally the discoloration fades.

"Look at that," Irma says. "All the stain has been cleansed away."

I know what she's trying to do. Make a big connection between my life with my father and this cloth.

"I'll just hang this up to dry now," I say, stepping away. There's a rack for the vestments on one wall of the sacristy, and I carefully drape the linen there. "I'm done for the day, I think."

She knows I'm not up for Father Stephen, or a forgiveness talk, or to mend the bond with my family. But Irma's good at saying her piece and then letting things go.

We walk together back to the office so I can gather my things.

I nod at her. "I'll be back in a few days."

She waves. "Mindy will be here on Thursday."

"Usual time?"

"Usual time."

My little white car gleams in the sun. It's already really hot, as summer has come in earnest. School has let out and a few children run along the sidewalk, followed by a distracted mother looking at her phone.

I drive slowly down the street, past my family's house. Mom's minivan isn't there. No one's home. I'm tempted to walk up and peer in the windows. Take a good look at my old life.

But I resist.

The park is next, the peeling equipment and patchy dying grass. I do stop here, pulling up alongside the curb.

There's a lot of memories to sort in this space. Recess with Andy. Walks with Mindy. Mom reading her book. Dad checking up on me.

And of course Blitz. We met here more than once.

As I get out of my car and walk through the trees, I wish I could figure out exactly what is going on with me so I could work at it, scrub myself free of it like that linen stain.

But it's a low nagging ache. And I can't break free.

A few kids run amok on the sidewalks and a pair of mothers sit conspiratorially on a bench, one of them burping a baby.

I don't know why I'm here. I should be looking ahead, not behind.

So I go back to my car. I purposely turn away from Dreamcatcher Dance Academy so I don't have to drive by it and face my memories there. As I head back to my empty house, I get a message from Blitz.

I wait until I'm in the garage to take out my phone.

Hey, call me when you get this. You won't believe the message Hannah just got.

Hannah is Blitz's manager. Well, sort of. We can't

fire her due to the contract, but we don't work directly with her anymore. He has his assistant Shelly be the go-between.

As I walk into the house, I wonder what could be up. The new season of *Dance Blitz* won't start filming for months. They are still auditioning contestants for Mack. There shouldn't be anything to do, unless some other show wants Blitz to come on, or both of us.

When I've kicked off my shoes and am ensconced on the sofa, I dial Blitz's number.

His voice makes me smile. "Princess! Sorry, I mean, Livia! You will never guess what has happened!"

I regret snapping at him for calling me Princess. He's done it since the day we met.

"Let me guess," I say, trying to sound upbeat. "You and Giselle are going to host a new dance show together."

Giselle was the trampy *Dance Blitz* finalist who went a little crazy when she got eliminated.

"Good one. And ugh. No way. This is about you! The casting director for Dominika Sokolov wants you to come to a rehearsal tomorrow at Jenica's!"

"Wait. What? Who is Dominika whatever you said?"

"That Russian ballerina who is going on tour. The one Jenica talked about!"

"I didn't audition for that."

"You don't have to. Their scout saw you and wants you to come." Blitz's voice sounds like he is literally resting on cloud nine.

"But he didn't even look at me. The other girls were much better."

"Doesn't matter. He wants you."

My fingers run along the velvety surface of the sofa. "Do I have to?"

Blitz is quiet. In that empty space, I picture him rubbing his eyes, unsure of what to do with a sad, mopey girlfriend who doesn't want to buy a house or take advantage of an incredible opportunity to dance.

"Well, just think about it. I can come back tonight and go with you tomorrow. Shelly can get me on a red-eye."

I don't know what to say. That I don't have the energy. That I don't want to go on tour, strange people, strange cities, strange everything.

"You know what," he says, "I'm going to go ahead and get on a plane as soon as the show is over. I'll be there before you wake up." Blitz's energy hasn't slowed down. "It won't hurt to just go check it out."

He's right. I can put on my big-girl leotard and at least be considerate of their interest. It's what you do in show business, no matter what form it takes. This is what I signed on for when I chose Blitz.

"Okay. I'll see you then."

"Terrific! We'll have to find you an agent. We definitely don't want both of us tied up with the Evil One."

I manage a short laugh. "That's for sure."

"I love you, Livia," he says. "I'm super proud of you."

This makes my throat form a lump. "Thank you, Blitz. I love you too."

I set the phone on the floor and fall back on the cushions. I'm going to have to pull myself together.

And if I'm dancing tomorrow with real ballerinas, then I better get my butt off the sofa and practice.

Chapter Nine

✦

Blitz does make it back by the next morning. Despite his late night, he's practically bouncing with excitement as I pack a dance bag for the rehearsal.

"Do you think you'll get a solo? Will some hunky ballet boy get to dance with you? Will they put you on the posters?" He keeps Googling other traveling ballet shows to see how they do top billing, how the ballerinas are chosen, and how much stage time each type of performer gets.

It doesn't matter to me. I'm not sure I even want to do this. But the idea of being an actual ballerina has a lot of pull. It's enough to get me out of the house and thinking about a future full of good what-ifs, not the lost ones.

The small parking lot at Jenica's is jam-packed, cars lined up on the street for blocks. Blitz pulls up to drop me off and promises to return as soon as he can find a place to leave the car.

"We should have called Ted," I say. We haven't seen him in days.

"I'll be right there," Blitz says as I open the door. "Don't run off with the ballet until I'm there to kiss you good-bye!"

I shake my head. As if that would happen.

Inside, the foyer is packed with people. A different girl is at Weeza's makeshift desk. "Aren't you lovely!" she says with a friendly tilt of her head. "Name?"

Total change from Weeza, for sure.

"Livia Mason," I say. "Or it might say Livia Mays. That's my stage name."

The girl lifts her eyebrows, then looks me straight in the face. "Hey, you're that girl from *Dance Blitz*!" She stands up. "Dmitri! Livia is up here!"

I can't see anybody in the craziness of dancers in leotards, coaches, and general people who ordinarily come to Jenica's. I wonder if anybody's in the gym.

But the crowd starts to part, and I see the man from the other day. He's dressed up today in a white button-down shirt and khakis. He smiles at me and waves as he moves forward.

"Livia," he says, grasping my hand in both of his. "I'm so glad you made it."

"I heard you tracked me down," I say. "I'm not sure I'm really a good candidate for this."

"Of course you are," he says. "The whole world has watched you do ballet. You have more fans than the biggest, most prima ballerina in all the stage!"

Blitz bursts through the door, and stops short when he sees me so close. "Hey!"

"You remember Blitz, I'm sure," I say. "Blitz, this is Dmitri."

Only now does Dmitri release my hand to shake Blitz's. "A real pleasure."

"Love that accent," Blitz says. "How long have you been in the States?"

"About six months," Dmitri says. "We've been securing funding for the tour."

"I'm always looking for great acts to produce," Blitz says. "Especially when they include Livia."

Dmitri raises his eyebrows. "We will keep that in mind."

"I haven't agreed to do it yet!" I say to Blitz.

"Of course," Blitz says. "So what is happening here today?"

Another girl comes through the door, so we step away from the desk to let her sign in.

"We have already held the initial auditions,"

Dmitri says. "Today the dancers who made the first cut will learn one of the numbers, and we will cut more."

"I'm totally going to get cut," I say. "I don't have near the ballet experience that most of these girls do."

Dmitri shakes his head. "Humility. I see so little of it in this work."

"Isn't she great?" Blitz says.

That's as far as the conversation gets, as one of the girls says, "Isn't that Blitz Craven?"

And we're mobbed.

Blitz smiles and signs dance bags and random slips of paper the girls dig out. We're obviously not in Kansas anymore. Jenica's normal crew would never do that.

We're saved by a ringing sound that gets everyone quiet.

Jenica calls out, "All dancers need to report to the gym to get your numbers and line up for the first rehearsal."

This draws everyone away from Blitz and through the doors to the gym.

I start to head that way, but Dimitri catches my arm. "You stay with me a little longer. There is no need for you to take a number. Once the others are settled, we will go in and you can see the style and breadth of the dance. If you enjoy the music and would like to know more, we can talk away from here."

"So I'm not auditioning?" I ask.

"No," Dmitri says. "A position is yours for the taking."

Blitz slides his arm around my waist. "What position is that?"

"Livia would be what we call a Guest Artist, a highly regarded ballerina engaged for the tour."

"Would she be on the poster?" Blitz asks.

"Blitz!" I exclaim. "This isn't a movie."

Dmitri smiles. "It is fine, all good questions. Livia would be considered a very valuable asset for drawing large audiences across the States. She would have second billing only to Dominika herself."

I wonder if this Russian ballerina will be annoyed at having to share the spotlight with a third-year ballet student who only has six months in toe shoes. And many of those spent on the sofa.

"This sounds great," Blitz says. "Should we go in?"

"Let's see where they are," Dmitri says.

We follow him to one of the doors to the gym. Inside, the dancers are pinning numbers to their leotards and the girl who was at the door is checking their names against their numbers.

Two women and a man stand in front of the line

of dancers, talking and doing an occasional dance move.

In the corner, Conner, who often runs the music here, sits at the tiny soundboard that controls the speakers.

I look around for Jenica and finally spot her sitting in the back corner on a pile of mats. Next to her is an incredibly poised and regal-looking woman in a pink leotard, with white-blond hair piled elegantly on her head.

"Is that Dominika?" I ask Dmitri. "In the corner on the mat?"

Dmitri nods. "She stands out, doesn't she? She is as beautiful as a dove, as graceful as a swan."

Blitz grimaces behind Dmitri's back, and I almost giggle.

"Why did she leave Russia?" I ask. "Or is that public knowledge?"

Dmitri frowns. "It did not make the news here, I don't think. Her father was a diplomat. Her mother was a great gymnast. They were thrown from a hotel balcony."

I suck in a breath. "What? Why?"

Dmitri shrugs. "Those are matters of state. But Dominika no longer has the heart for her country. So she came here."

I watch the elegant woman talk to Jenica. She sits

tall and proud, but I see the seriousness in her. I think about what I have lost and realize that is nothing. Gabriella will grow up and can see me when she is eighteen, if she wants.

And my parents aren't dead. Just shell-shocked. Maybe they will one day realize how they have overreacted.

I still have hope for seeing my family again. Dominika does not.

"Let's go inside," Dmitri says. "It looks as though they are about to start the choreography."

Blitz, Dmitri, and I walk in. We do not go to the corner with Jenica and Dominika, but settle on the edge of one of the trampolines, which have been pushed against the wall. I'm fine with this. I'm not sure I'm ready to meet a prima ballerina in person yet.

The three coaches spread out and lead a warm-up. Only now that I'm settled do I notice that Weeza is out there. I elbow Blitz. "Look," I say. "Three from the end."

"Weeza," Blitz says. "She got new tights for the occasion."

He's right. She's traded her slashed tights for new plain black ones. Her hair is slicked back today, not in tight blond pigtails all over her head.

"Who knew she could be classy?" Blitz says.

"She must be pretty good to make the first cut," I say.

"Have you ever seen her dance?" he asks. "I haven't."

I shake my head. "Not once. Maybe she waits until after the normal hours."

"Maybe we scare her off."

We watch the dancers go through mostly traditional exercises. You start to see the difference in their training when in some of the ballet positions, a few of the dancers have different arm placement. They quickly conform to the coaches.

"Wait. The five positions aren't universal?" Blitz asks.

"There are some slight variations," Dmitri says. "It is not important."

"People doing the basics differently isn't important?" Blitz is clearly troubled with this.

"They are only the foundations," Dmitri says. "It's the form that matters."

The dancers start working on the first sequence of the dance.

"What ballet is this?" I ask.

"You Americans know it as *Sleeping Beauty*," Dmitri says. "It is one of three ballets by Tchaikovsky, the others, of course, being *The Nutcracker* and *Swan Lake*."

"What role are you thinking of for Livia?" Blitz asks.

"It has not been discussed at great length just yet. I only discovered your Livia last week," Dmitri says.

I want to protest the "your Livia" but let it go as a cultural or language issue. I lean forward, my elbows on my knees, certain I don't look even in the ballpark of Dominika's grace or poise.

"Does the ballet have three fairies like the movie?" Blitz asks. "Livia should be the blue one."

Dmitri laughs. "There are many fairies in the ballet. But only one important one, the..." He hesitates. "It is purple, not the bright one."

"Lilac," I say.

"Yes, the Lilac Fairy," Dmitri says. "And of course there is Carabosse, the evil fairy."

I turn to the boys now. "Can I be evil?"

Dmitri's lips curl into a sardonic smile. "You are ready for a change of image, yes? Perhaps. We would review the technical aspects of the dance, and see if they fit your style and abilities."

My gaze goes back to the dancers. Some are obviously nervous, concentrating fiercely, struggling to keep up. I feel badly for them, doubly so because I'm sitting here on my butt, being offered parts with no effort at all.

So strange how life goes.

"I'd love to go for the evil fairy," I say.

Dmitri claps his hands. "I will talk to Ivana," he says. "We will see how you do and if it is a good fit. I'm sure she can get you ready."

"When does the ballet begin?" Blitz asks.

"This is our last audition stop," Dmitri says. "We've already been to New York, Boston, and Miami. Rehearsals start in two weeks."

"Where will those be?" Blitz asks.

"Chicago, actually," Dmitri says. "One of our producers is lending us his space for the six weeks of rehearsals."

Blitz glances over at me. I know what he's thinking. Six weeks in Chicago. If he should come, or if he'd be in the way.

"And the tour?" he asks.

"Thirty shows in eight cities." Dmitri rubs his hands together. "It will be a grand occasion."

"So another, what, three months?" Blitz asks.

"Thereabouts," Dmitri says. "It's a six-month commitment."

Blitz nods his head, but he's looking down. I wonder if this is hard for him to think about. He's definitely less excited than he was.

What do I want?

It's a novel thing to think about. I had years of my father's rule, then running to do the show, wandering around based on what life was throwing at me.

Now I can just...choose.

I shift my gaze to watch the dancers move through their roles. A few of them are called from the line and cut. One girl's eyes tear up as she plucks her number from her leotard.

Disappointment. I know it well.

But being evil has a nice ring to it.

Chapter Ten

I work like crazy the next week. We hire a private ballet teacher and rent a small studio, far from both Dreamcatcher and Jenica's. This gives me the distance I need to focus.

We watch various versions of the *Sleeping Beauty* ballet and work on my general ability to act and portray a character as well as dance. The director of the new ballet will determine how to portray the evil fairy, but I don't want to be caught so off guard that I'm not even in the ballpark.

Mostly, I stay *en pointe* as many hours a day as I can without injuring myself. It's the hardest work I've ever done, but it's better to do it now while I'm still on my own than later, when I have a room full of ballerinas who wanted my role watching me for mistakes and weakness.

My feet start looking like a real ballerina's, covered in callouses and blisters, the nails bruised and short. I'm embarrassed by them, but Blitz is so impressed by my dedication that they become badges of honor.

By the time Dmitri calls us to a staff meeting, I feel better about doing a ballet. It only remains to be seen what they will offer me and if I will take it.

And then there is Blitz. For over half a year now, we've been together constantly other than brief trips. This is a long haul. Six months on the road for me. I don't know if he'll stay behind or come along. I doubt I'll have much time for him, as my life will be a lot like when we were rehearsing and filming *Dance Blitz*.

Our plans to negotiate as a team go up in smoke when a big talk show, one of the biggest, has a cancellation and wants Blitz to fill the last-minute slot. It's an incredible opportunity for him, a shot he's dreamed of. But it falls on the same day as the staff meeting for *Sleeping Beauty*.

He hesitates, but I refuse to let him, assuring him I can handle negotiations on my own. He regrets not getting me an agent before now. I promise not to sign any papers without sending them to his lawyer, Larry.

And he's off.

I'm pretty nervous, so instead of driving myself, I call Ted to take me to the hotel where Dmitri and Dominika are staying.

Ted drives Blitz's red Ferrari now, and when he arrives in it, I decide to sit up front, like I did when Blitz and I were first together.

"I hope it's not too flashy," Ted says.

"It's fine," I tell him. "Maybe it will bring me good luck."

"You seem to have all the luck you need," he says as we head through the back streets to the freeway.

He doesn't know what happened with Gwen and Gabriella. Or my family. It's always easy to see the fun parts. The fame. Money. Stardom. And it's true that I'm probably about to be handed something other girls will work hard for and never get.

I stare out the window. San Antonio zooms by. The reasons to stay here are gone now. Gwen won't let me see my daughter. I can't dance at Dreamcatcher. Maybe this is the right thing. See more cities. Make a new home. I guess I was right to hesitate on buying a house.

At church, Irma always says that when God closes a door, He always opens a window.

This ballet just might be the window.

Ted pulls through the valet circle and stops in front of the gold and glass entrance. "Go get 'em," he says.

A porter opens my door. I step out uncertainly, already forgetting which meeting room I'm supposed to go to.

I walk slowly through the main doors, fiddling with my phone to find the email that lists the location.

A woman's voice calls out, "Livia?"

I look up. It's Juliet, the professional ballerina who often comes to Dreamcatcher Academy to help with classes. She is the daughter of the owner, Danika, and the wife of Bennett, who was one of the *Dance Blitz* producers who got Blitz started in the business. She also helped me the night I walked onto the finale of the show.

I'm so glad to see her I could cry. I hurriedly catch up to her. She's lovely in a soft white sundress, her black hair falling down her back.

"Are you going to be in the ballet?" I ask.

"Oh, no, I'm under contract," she says. "But Blitz called Bennett to see if he could recommend someone to help you with this negotiation since he had to leave, and Bennett thought I could help."

She envelops me in a hug that smells of lavender. I'm so glad she's here. My nerves are completely calmed knowing she will be helping me.

"He didn't tell me!" I exclaim.

Juliet leads us to the elevators across the atrium. "I just found out myself a half hour ago. I had to throw on some clothes and get over here!"

"Thank you," I say. "I have no idea what I'm doing!"

The elevator dings and the door slides open.

We step inside.

"It sounds like they are bringing you on as a guest ballerina. Usually those roles are a little less taxing than some of the others. There are many fun but minor roles in *Sleeping Beauty*. There's an entire cast of storybook characters at the end."

"I was hoping for the evil fairy."

Juliet nods. "That's a primary role. But it can be a dancing role or just an acting role."

"Have you done the ballet?"

"Yes, we toured Eastern Europe with it two years ago."

"Did you have a role?"

"I was Princess Florine. She dances with Bluebird at the wedding in the third act. It's a nice minor role. A *pas de deux* and a short solo."

I couldn't even imagine getting a bigger role than someone like Juliet. She's been a professional ballerina for years. Maybe I shouldn't negotiate for that. It's too much. I watch the numbers change on the elevator display, thinking.

"Is there a different part I should do, then?" I ask her.

"There are nice roles with only small amounts of dancing, especially in the prologue and the wedding. You could be a secondary fairy. Or one of the storybook characters. They are fun."

"You think I shouldn't dance much?"

"Well," she says, "it's more an issue of overtaxing your body and getting injured. You don't have a lot of years behind you. It's a distinct disadvantage."

The elevator slows to a stop. "You know where we're going?" I ask.

"The lounge on the top floor," she says.

"Have you done meetings like this?" I ask.

"Not personally. I belong to a specific company where roles are cast internally. But certainly in some of the touring ballets, they work to get big names and there are negotiations like what you're about to do."

We walk down the hall to the end. A pair of double doors are thrown open, and inside is an expansive room filled with sofas and armchairs.

In the corner formed by two enormous windows is a long meeting table. Four people sit there, including Dmitri. I don't see Dominika.

Dmitri stands. "Livia, how lovely to see you!" He reaches for my hand. Instead of shaking it, though, he brings it to his lips for a quick kiss. "This must be Juliet Claremont. Thank you for letting me know you were coming to assist Livia."

He kisses her hand as well, then says, "Please, let me introduce you."

We take seats at the end of the table.

"This is Alexei Baryshnikov," Dmitri says. "He is an expatriate like most of us and serves as our founding patron." He gestures to an elderly man with bright eyes beneath bushy white brows. His hair is so white and thick, it almost appears to be a wig.

He nods at us. "Pleasure," he says.

Dimitri points at two women on the opposite side, their fair hair lit by the big windows. "This is Ivana. I spoke of her. She is our primary choreographer. We brought her with us from Russia."

Ivana gives a small wave but does not smile.

"And this is Evangeline. We hired her in Miami to lead the auditions and training, as well as to work with the corps ballerinas."

Evangeline is blond and has a dancer's poise. "Nice to meet you," she says. She is more stiff than Ivana, and I sense her appraising me as if I don't quite meet her standards.

"We have a few other instructors and trainers," Dmitri explains. "But it was not necessary to bring them here."

"Have most of the casting decisions been made?" Juliet asks.

Alexei speaks. "We have a preliminary list," he says. "We know the makeup of most of the corps, the King and Queen and some incidental non-dancing roles. Dominika will play Aurora, of course. And we have a very talented gentleman in the role of the Prince."

"Have you cast the minor fairies?" Juliet asks. "Or

the storybook characters?"

"Some of them," Dmitri says. "Puss in Boots is cast. Cinderella. Bluebird. Two fairies."

"What are you looking at for Livia?" Juliet asks.

The table is quiet. Evangeline cuts her eyes to the choreographer, Ivana. Alexei holds on to the polished top of an intricate cane that rests between his knees.

"There is some concern," Dmitri says carefully, "that any larger role would be too much for a ballerina of your..." he falters, as if his English is not providing him the sensitive words he needs. "Tender early training. It is my understanding you are only six months *en pointe*."

"She is," Juliet says. "But she is a well-rounded dancer. She is up for whatever role will place her in the prominence you need to be able to use her celebrity as a publicity tool. She can't exactly go on talk shows as a courtier or a corps ballerina."

"We doubt she could even keep up with the corps," Ivana says quickly. "It's very technical and requires her form match the others."

I try not to squirm. It's the same sort of thing that was said about me in the *Dance Blitz* meetings. No one ever has any faith in what I can do.

But I am new. I am not a career dancer. I didn't start when I was four. And I've certainly never had to do ballet all day long, week after week.

Alexei speaks next, both hands on the cane. "We

want her to dance. If we want her to be part of the publicity, she has to dance."

"You would like to be Carabosse, is that right, Livia?" Dmitri asks.

All eyes are on me now.

"It does look like a fun role," I say.

Ivana stands up, her face blazing red. "We agreed Carabosse would not be an old hag stumbling around the stage! We agreed it before I signed on! We wanted a beautiful Carabosse who would dance like the other fairies!"

"Sit, sit, Ivana," Dmitri says. "No one is going to take away from your vision."

"But she has no experience!" Ivana says. She plunks back down in the chair. "She can't possibly do a solo. She won't hold up to the standards of the other dancers. We will have to scale the choreography way back."

Juliet slides her hands forward on the table to get the others' attention. "We may be underestimating her," Juliet says. "You have not even watched her dance more than a television number. I have seen Livia dance for this entire two years, and I believe that while she is young in her training, she has a lot of talent."

She turns directly to Ivana. "And matching a dancer's skill to her role is what great choreographers do."

Ivana sits back in her chair, her dark eyes blazing. With the sun lighting up her hair, she looks like an angry ghost. "I say White Cat. It's a cute role. Lots of character. Less technical than what we planned for the prologue."

"Now, now, Ivana," Alexei says. "Nobody even knows White Cat is in the ballet. People will say, 'What role is that?' Making her the evil fairy aligns her with Maleficent, and will make a wonderful poster with her behind Aurora."

"I come from a place where the dance is more important than marketing, Alexei," Ivana says sharply.

"Well, I will remind you that without an audience, we have no dance," Alexei retorts. He stamps his cane on the hardwood floor. "You will work with Livia and find the best use of her technique. Carabosse does not dance with the corps, so it is fine for her style to be less technical than theirs. Any deficiencies she has can be played off as in character."

Dmitri leans forward, bracing his elbows on the table. His perfectly groomed brows offset his light gleaming eyes. "Keep in mind that it is Aurora they will judge the dancing by. Carabosse is about the story."

Ivana crosses her arms over her chest. She has nothing more to say, it seems.

"Can she even act?" Evangeline asks. "We were very rigorous with the auditions for the acting roles!"

Everyone turns to me. My throat goes dry. This is worse than I imagined.

"I was able to play nice with Giselle," I say.

This gets a snort from Evangeline. "I can't believe you stood on the same stage with her."

"I wanted to push her offstage most of the time, but I did what needed to be done for the audience," I say.

Juliet leans forward. "Trust me when I tell you that Hollywood is more brutal than even the most horrible ballet rivalry. If Livia can survive that brutal schedule and live broadcasts and hold up through three months of ten-hour rehearsals and filming, she can do this."

Ivana lets out a long annoyed breath.

Dmitri and Alexei smile and nod at each other.

"You're forgetting a rather important point," Evangeline says.

"I know," Dmitri says. "I'll handle it."

Alexei grunts with annoyance.

Juliet looks back and forth at the two men. "Which is?"

Ivana puts on her first smile of the meeting. "Dominika has final approval on all casting. If she says Livia isn't good enough, she's not good enough."

Great.

Chapter Eleven

I get surprise visitors at the condo that afternoon. Juliet and Bennett arrive to watch the talk show Blitz is on, dragging with them two of my instructor friends from Dreamcatcher Dance Academy.

Jacob comes in first, looking around our place with his eye for details. "Girl, you two have GOT to get a decorator in here," he says. He looks perfectly put together in my admittedly drab living room, wearing shiny silver pants and a vivid purple shirt with a scarf tucked inside the open upper buttons.

"It's just a rental," I tell him. "We've been trying to find a house."

"Have you?" Aurora says. She looks completely different without several toddlers in tutus hanging on her legs. Her flowery shirt is ruffled and off the shoulder, and her hair is down. I don't think I've ever seen her dark hair outside a tight dance bun.

Bennett and Juliet have brought a basket of cheese and grapes and wine. Bennett organizes it all on the coffee table while Jacob looks over the back-yard. "It's totally hot enough to go skinny-dipping later. That pool is delish."

This makes Bennett pause and look over at Juliet with an expression that conveys "What have you gotten me into?"

Her laughter is bright. "You go right ahead, Jacob. Maybe Livia can publish a picture to Blitz's Twitter feed and you can have your fifteen minutes of fame."

Jacob turns to me. "Would you do that for me, Livia?" he asks, his voice all sincere, but his eyes dancing with amusement.

"It would just get all the women after you," I say.

He waves his hand as if dismissing the idea. "Blitz has a gay demographic. I mean, look at *moi*."

Bennett picks up a remote and looks around. "I assume you have a television tucked away some-where," he says. "I didn't think to ask about that."

The four of them glance around, as if just now realizing there isn't a TV or a cabinet large enough to house one anywhere.

I let them wonder for a moment, then tell Bennett, "Push the auxiliary button at the bottom."

He looks skeptical but pushes it.

A door swings down from the ceiling with a mechanical buzz, then a projector screen begins to descend. It's broad and bright white, covering half the width of the wall behind it.

"Holy Mother of sweet technology," Jacob breathes.

"You can power it all on now," I say.

Bennett peers at the remote, then a blue rectangle of light flashes across the white screen.

"That is cool," Aurora says. She plunks down on the brown leather sofa.

The system is in DVD mode, so I take the remote and switch it to pick up television stations.

"We have ten minutes," Juliet says.

I whip through the channels until I find the right one. The evening news is still on.

"Steer me to the kitchen and I'll find plates and glasses," Bennett says.

I walk with him into the next room. It's still funny to me to think of this billionaire businessman serving snacks to my friends. Maybe he was always this laid back. But I'm guessing Juliet has something to do with it.

We load up with plates and cloth napkins and wine glasses and return to the living room.

"They're doing a teaser for the show!" Juliet says.

And there he is, Blitz himself, waving as the voice-over talks about the lineup for the evening.

"He looks amazing," Jacob says.

And he does. He's wearing slim black dance pants and a pale gray button-down with the sleeves rolled up, a black vest over it. He looks both Hollywood and Texas. I wonder who dressed him, if his manager Hannah got a say or if it was one of the stylists from *Dance Blitz*.

As far as I know, no one talks to Hannah other than Blitz's assistant Shelly. Blitz won't speak to her after she orchestrated the ambush by the three finalists that led to us doing five episodes of *Dance Blitz* together.

Although now that it's over, I have to admit, I had fun working with him and seeing the inside of a reality show. I hope they aren't going to surprise him with anything tonight.

Jacob must be having the same line of thought. "You don't think they'll bring on that Giselle girl again, do you?" he says. "She's disappeared into the black hole of Hollywood has-beens."

"It was super-short notice," I say. "They couldn't have practiced a dance number or planned something crazy."

"Let's hope not," Juliet says. "You two have had enough of that."

Bennett sits next to her on the love seat that angles away from the sofa where Jacob and Aurora have ensconced themselves.

"Has Blitz mentioned anything to you about what he's doing on the show?" Bennett asks. "They should have had a rehearsal."

I check my phone. "Not since he said they were about to meet to review the plan," I say. "That was hours ago."

"Busy getting prepped," Juliet says. "It can be hectic."

I settle onto the overstuffed cushion of an armchair as I try to relax. It will just be a chitchat show, nothing more.

I hope.

A text comes through, and the whole room turns to me as I pull my phone out of my pocket.

"Is it him?" Aurora asks.

It is. I read it quickly and say, "He just says that rehearsal went fine. He is doing a short dance number based on one we did last season, nothing fancy, just him so he can ad lib if he needs to, and that they are focusing on the changes to *Dance Blitz* and where he's headed next."

"Good," Juliet says. "That's exactly what it should be."

The commercials end and the opening screen of the talk show comes on.

"Is he first billing?" Jacob asks. "He should be first billing."

The host of the show steps out for a short monologue. Blitz isn't first billing. An actress is up for the initial segment. Then Blitz will dance and talk.

When the show is back in commercial, Bennett passes out plates. "Eat, drink, and be merry," he says. "For tomorrow is a workday."

I accept the plate Jacob hands me, although I don't feel particularly hungry. I'm glad they are here, though.

"How did negotiations go today?" Bennett asks.

"Negotiations?" Jacob pipes in. "What new thing is on Livia's horizon?"

"A ballet," I say, popping a sliver of cheese in my mouth. "*Sleeping Beauty*."

"You would be a divine Aurora," Jacob says. "It's about time she wasn't blond."

I shake my head. "Oh, no, I'm not experienced enough for that."

"I'll say," Aurora says. "Being Aurora is hard!"

We all laugh at the irony of her saying that.

"I know," I tell her. "I've asked to be Carabosse."

"Girlfriend, who is that?" Jacob asks.

"The evil fairy who curses Aurora," Aurora says. "Haven't you watched any classical ballet?"

"Only when you do it," he says.

"You jazz dancers," she teases. "Never learning anything classic."

"Baby girl, you don't even want to get me started on your gaps in dance knowledge," he shoots back, but there is no meanness to it. I can tell it's a conversation they have often.

I had forgotten they were such tight friends. Generally at the academy, I only see them separately, but now I remember people mentioning that sometimes Jacob and Aurora do contemporary dance together at a small theater on the Riverwalk.

I bet they're amazing. I should ask around the academy and find out when they perform.

Except.

I can't go there anymore to ask.

"How is Danika?" I ask. "Summer sign-ups good?"

Jacob and Aurora glance at each other.

"Lots of toddlers like always," Aurora says carefully. "You know how it is after school is out. Fewer weekly classes, more weeklong camps."

"How are the wheelchair ballerinas?" I hate to ask, but I am desperate to know if Gwen brought Gabriella back after I left.

Another glance between the two of them.

"I'm sure the class will come back in the fall," Aurora says.

My chest tightens. "You mean it's gone?" I can't believe it. All the work to get it filled. For nothing.

"It was a small, specialized class," Aurora says. "Those almost always go on hiatus during the summer." She reaches over to squeeze my arm. "They'll come back."

But not Gabriella. I'm sure she's gone for good.

"It's on again!" Juliet calls out.

The host sits behind his desk. Behind him, scenes from *Dance Blitz* flash on a large screen. Blitz on a date with Giselle, then one of the big numbers from the live finale, and a brief glimpse of the sexy dance he and I did during the last season.

My face heats up to see myself, even if only for a few seconds, in that revealing getup. I have avoided watching the show since it aired earlier this year.

"Put your hands together for the man, the wild one, the dancing beast, Blitz Craven!" the host says, standing behind his desk.

The camera pans to the entertainment stage, and there is Blitz, smoke rising on either side of him, frozen in place, looking down, a roguish hat tugged low on his forehead.

The band behind him fires up and he spins, a crazy whirlwind, endlessly long, until it seems like there is no way anyone could come out of it without losing their balance.

The crowd screams as he stops in a dramatic freeze, then rushes into a high-energy number that is a mix of jazz and breakdancing.

"He's killing it," Jacob says. "I wish I had half his moves."

It's true. My heart surges watching him. Way too

soon, the song smashes to a halt and Blitz freezes one last time. The audience goes crazy.

The host stands up to clap for him. So does the actress.

Blitz heads over to the sofa and desk. The actress moves down to give Blitz the spot closer to the host. He's still breathing hard.

"Man! That was outrageous." The host looks out. "Was that amazing or what?"

The audience volume reaches a fever pitch.

Blitz nods and waves them off. This is different from how he used to be, hamming it up, jumping around, sparking them into a frenzy.

He sits down, leaning forward, still catching his breath.

The talk settles in, the ending of the show, the new bachelor for *Dance Blitz*.

Bennett pours more wine and we all relax. It's going the way it should. This isn't some dramatic morning show where they have surprise visits by ex-girlfriends or startling confrontations.

Blitz gets up and dances with the actress, who stumbles a bit and makes fun of herself and her awkwardness. It's charming and sweet.

When they sit down again, a new image flashes onscreen behind them, and I instantly go on alert.

"What are they gonna do?" Jacob says, sitting forward on the sofa.

It's a picture of me and the three finalists from *Dance Blitz*. After a moment, everyone fades out except Giselle.

"You hearing from this girl much, Blitz?" the host asks.

"Not a word," Blitz says. "Everyone has moved on to the next thing."

"Giselle had a bit of a meltdown on her last episode, didn't she?"

"She wasn't expecting to be eliminated before the final two," Blitz says. "I'm sure she'll go on to have a great career."

He looks wary, as if he expects them to spring Giselle on him. That girl is still a sore spot in his career. Giselle has a decent following, and they tried to get an audit of the votes when she was eliminated. That went nowhere, of course. Nobody said the show was a democracy.

"We have a little video for you," he says.

Blitz doesn't answer, and despite his easy expression, I can see the tension in his jaw, his arms crossed over the vest.

The screen behind them switches over to a video. It's Giselle, in selfie mode, holding a phone camera.

"Hey, Blitz!" she says, as if it's live. "I'm here on the set of *Dancing with the Stars*, and everyone thinks you and I should be contestants together!" She pans the camera a little, and the signature stage and logo light up behind her. "You haven't answered my calls, so I'm here to ask you in front of everybody — are you willing to dance with me?"

The video freezes with Giselle's plaintive expression.

The host turns to Blitz. "So what do you think?" he asks the audience. "You want to see Blitz and Giselle back together?"

There's decent applause and a few cheers.

"Oh, no, he totally won't do it," Jacob says.

"That girl is desperate," Aurora says. "And she put him on the spot."

I see Blitz slip into his old demeanor, shifting down on the sofa, looking out over the audience. He finds the hot camera and stares right at us. The cameraman zooms in.

"I have a great life," Blitz says. "And I'm spending it with Livia."

The crowd claps louder for this. I watch Blitz, his expression earnest. He really knows how to work a camera. It's how he charmed huge numbers of viewers on his show.

But right now, I can tell he's thinking of me. He knows I'm looking. And he's speaking right to me.

He's really walked away from all that. No talk show host or silly video or audience reaction could change his mind.

He's here for *me*.

Chapter Twelve

I'm on pins and needles as we wait to hear the final word from the ballet. I'm not sure I'll even take it. Blitz has turned down gigs left and right to stay with me. Anything longer than a couple days for a talk show or a guest appearance is an automatic no.

We call off the search for a house here in San Antonio. He agrees that it's not as necessary as it once was, when we were teaching Gabriella and planning our lives around her.

But I can't stop thinking about the situation.

I have Gwen's address. I've always had it, at least in the two years since I first found her. It's the first thing I knew other than their names. I found it in an old-fashioned phone book.

When I was younger, I would sometimes call the number secretly from church, then hang up if Gwen or her husband answered. Once I heard a child singing in the background and it was literally the best day ever.

Until I got my license a few weeks ago, driving somewhere alone wasn't an option. I couldn't truly sneak around.

But now I can.

This is why, one afternoon after my private ballet workout, I sit alone in my car and pull out Google Maps. I tap in the address I've had memorized since I was seventeen.

It's a bit of a drive, maybe half an hour from where I am right now. Blitz might wonder why I'm late, but he won't question me. I'm not exactly the sort of girl who might be doing something wrong.

Is this wrong?

I guess so. Stalking.

My little white convertible pulls away from the curb. The Google voice tells me to get on the freeway, but I am too nervous for that still. When I stay on the frontage road and take a different artery through town, it adjusts.

It's just a peek, right? I'll see what sort of house my baby girl lives in. Maybe catch sight of a toy or two in the yard, and know a bit more about her other than her love of brightly colored tutus and ribbon sticks.

It strikes me how narrow my view of her has

been. Gabriella has always seemed happy, but she loves dance. Maybe in other situations she cries, or whines, and maybe Gwen has to scold her.

I picture this and my stomach twists. No, I won't think of it. Gabriella is cheerful, even when she has trouble. She once got a blister on her thumb from dancing in the wheelchair, before Gwen realized she would need gloves for dance.

Despite the bleeding painful sore, Gabriella didn't cry over it more than the first few seconds after it popped. A Band-Aid and a hug cured her completely and she went on, adjusting by holding the wheel a different way.

And she had only been four years old.

No, I know her. I do. She's tough and strong and sweet.

The best.

My eyes smart now. I shouldn't do this. I should not invade her world or drown myself in what-ifs. I should turn my car around and go home.

But I don't.

I cross through middle-class neighborhoods, cars parked on the street and bikes lying across driveways. In the cul-de-sacs, there are basketball hoops, sometimes with kids playing at them. It's summer. Time for fun.

The voice guides me through turns and down streets. I pass restaurants, a bowling alley, two grocery stores. I wonder which of these places Gabriella has visited. I can see her rolling a heavy ball from the wheelchair, bouncing it off the guards until it finally makes it to the end.

I bowled in the time before my father shut down our family. Andy was too young, but some of the kids used a little ramp to send the ball down the lane.

I would do that with her. She would love it. Maybe Gwen has thought of it.

Does Gwen help her make the most of what she can do? She brought her to Dreamcatcher. The flier I mailed her with a stolen stamp worked. She looked for opportunities and took them. I have to believe Gabriella is the best she can be where she is.

I am close.

I turn down her street. My heart speeds up. What will I see? Gwen's white SUV, if it isn't in the garage. The front door. Maybe I will spot a neighbor or a friend.

I realize I'm not wearing sunglasses and fumble in the console to find them. They aren't there. I left them at home.

No scarf for my hair. What if they are sitting outside? What if they see me driving by?

They won't recognize the car. I never drove it to Dreamcatcher. The top is up. The windows are small.

I tell myself to breathe. The odds of them being outside their house are very low.

"The destination is on your left," Google tells me, and I slow down.

I was right, and there is no one in the yard or on the sidewalks.

Gwen's car is in the driveway.

I feel bold, and hit the brake to really take my time as I pass. It's a simple limestone house with green trim. Pretty front door. The wheelchair ramp is obviously newer than the porch, as the concrete is bright white compared to the rest.

No toys in the yard. Everything is neat.

Right as the view gets too far behind me to look anymore, I spot an interesting-looking swing in the tree. But I can't quite get a good peek. Did Gabriella swing there as a baby? Did they leave it because she still uses it, or because it is sentimental? Maybe the father hung it and Gwen can't bring herself to take it down.

But something about it is unusual, not typical for a baby swing. It seems too big. Maybe it's a special one for Gabriella to use.

I want to know.

At least this is what I tell myself as I circle the block and prepare to pass the house again. There was no one out. Nobody will notice a white car cruising by more than once.

This time, I approach from the other direction so

that Gwen's car won't block my view until I'm too close.

The blue swing is oversized and has a large black harness. If it's a baby swing, I've never seen one like it.

I'm so busy looking at it, that I'm passing the house by the time I realize one of the windows has purple curtains and a big flower sticker. Is that Gabriella's room?

There were other stickers. I want to know what they are. Does she love My Little Pony? Or Disney Princesses?

My desperation to see some little thing about her hits a peak.

One more pass, I tell myself. I will drive by one more time and then I will go home.

I make a bigger circle this time, so there will be a delay.

But as I approach the house, a message dings through from my phone to my car dash.

Everything going okay today?

It's Blitz.

I'm too close to stop and answer him. So I punch the message away and peer back at their house.

And almost scream.

They are outside, going down the ramp.

It's Gwen and Gabriella and a man, probably the new boyfriend she mentioned early this year.

I freak out so hard that I slam on my brakes.

It's the worst thing I could do.

My tires squeal a little on the pavement, making all three of them look up.

God, God, no no no.

I shield my eyes, hoping they can't see in the car very easily, and hit the gas.

I race away from their house, their neighborhood, their lives.

Never again, Livia, I tell myself.

You have to stay away.

But I'm crying even as I think it.

How can I? How can I give her up completely?

I don't know how to go on.

I should never have found her in the first place. Not knowing was so much easier than the pain of losing her a second time.

Chapter Thirteen

I don't tell Blitz what I did. We have dinner as usual, and he comes with me to ballet practice the next day. If he notices that I'm jittery or anxious after my close call running into Gwen, he doesn't bring it up.

I half expect a shoe to drop. For Danika to call, an anxious Gwen having let her know I was on her street.

But it never does.

We're halfway through the day with Amelia, the new ballet teacher, when my phone rings. My nerves are still on edge, so I hurry over to look at who it is.

It's Dmitri.

"Livia! Do you have a moment?"

I glance up at Blitz and Amelia. Blitz raises his eyebrows.

I mouth the word "Dmitri."

He gives me two thumbs-up, and he and Amelia head back to the mats.

"I do," I say.

"Dominika would like to do a rehearsal with you this week, if you are available. We want to assess how the two of you will look together in Act 1 where you give her the spindle to prick her finger."

"So we'll be dancing together in that scene? Sometimes it's just acted out."

"Yes, Ivana has this entire concept of how Carabosse should be. It's not unprecedented. Several versions have Carabosse as a dancing ballerina fairy. She scoffs at the versions that have a non-dancing hag."

"Okay," I say. "When can we do this?"

"Tomorrow, perhaps, or if that is too soon, then Thursday or Friday?"

I might as well get this over with. "Tomorrow is fine. At Jenica's?"

"No, we've reserved a more private place for the rehearsals. I'll send you the address."

"That sounds fine."

"Eight a.m., then?" Dmitri asks.

"I'll be there," I say.

"I look forward to seeing you together," he says.

I wish I did.

Blitz bounds over. "So what did he say?"

"I have a rehearsal with Dominika tomorrow to see if we fit together well in the parts."

Blitz grasps me by the waist and lifts me in the air. "This is so great! You'll be a real pro ballerina!"

He brings me down and turns in a circle with me against his chest. "I'm so proud of you, baby! I always knew you had that extra spark!"

Did he? I wasn't sure of it myself. But I've gone down this path now. I'll see it through.

THE NEXT MORNING, BLITZ AND I DRIVE OVER TO the new studio. It's on the opposite side of town, and by the time we white-knuckle it through traffic to be fifteen minutes late, I'm glad I have him with me.

"You run in," Blitz says as we pull up to the door. "I'll come in after I park."

I really, really hate being late. I'm the sort of person who shows up stupidly early to avoid the possibility. My hand fumbles with the handle as I jerk open the door and race inside.

It really is a small studio, only a tiny foyer the size of a closet that leads to the open door of the dance space.

Inside, Ivana is working with Dominika at the barre. Dmitri and Alexei sit in chairs in a back corner. Another girl works with Evangeline.

Dmitri stands. "Livia, so good of you to make it!"

Alexei waves from his chair as Dmitri comes forward.

Ivana and Dominika look up for a moment without smiling, then return to their work. I definitely feel the chill coming off them.

"Traffic was super bad," I say in a rush. "I'm so sorry to be late."

Dmitri waves the words away. "Do not trouble yourself. Just be on time to curtain calls!"

Ivana does speak up at that. "We pride ourselves on punctuality, Dmitri," she says. "Do not pamper the *TV star*."

The sneer on those last two words tells me all I need to know about how she feels.

I set my bag down and sit to change out of my Crocs. Dominika is in toe shoes, so I pull mine out as well.

Blitz rushes into the room, then stops short when he sees me on the floor. "Thought I'd stop in and hang," he says. The end of his sentence with its casual tone rings falsely in the stiff, formal room.

Ivana rolls her eyes. I can almost hear her thinking, "Uggh, these TV people."

"Good to see you again," Dmitri says, polite as always. "We shall find another chair for you with the rest of us observers."

"I'm good," Blitz says. "I can pull up some floor."

I focus on my shoes, getting them straight and tight. I love Blitz, but right now, he's adding to my anxiety.

"Evangeline, can you warm her up?" Ivana calls.

Evangeline turns to me with a frown. "I suppose that's more important than working with Angelique." There's a negative note that makes me grit my teeth.

"I can do my own warm-up," I say. "Just give me a few minutes."

"Eight a.m. means warm and ready at eight," Ivana says, shooting a glance at Dmitri. "For future reference."

"Got it," I say.

We're definitely not in Hollywood anymore. Nobody is going to be catering to us here.

Blitz's expression is dark now. He approaches to go through the warm-up with me. We have several stretches we are used to doing together.

When we both drop our heads to our knees, Blitz whispers, "They are drama queens."

I shrug. I was late. It's fair to call me out on it. Besides, every corner of the entertainment world has its issues. I put up with plenty when I had to work with the *Dance Blitz* finalists.

Suddenly I'm not sure I want this anymore.

"I'm thinking about walking out," I whisper.

Blitz squints one eye as he considers this. "A dramatic exit is a classic tactic."

"I'm not negotiating anymore. I'm outta here!" My voice rises a little at the end, and I hurriedly glance around to see if anyone has heard me.

Dmitri is watching us, but he's too far away to catch our conversation. The four girls are still deeply involved in their dance steps.

"Let's see how this goes," Blitz says. "Think of it as a social experiment between drama queens and rational people."

I sigh but nod. It would probably be poor judgment to burn this bridge.

We stand up and begin running through the basic positions, then spins and small leaps. We've done them together so many times that we are perfectly in sync.

When we finally pause, we discover everyone has stopped to watch us, even Ivana and Dominika.

Dmitri leans forward with a gleam in his eye, but Ivana squashes it quickly. "Male roles are cast," she says.

When he's about to say something else, she adds, "Even the corps. With backups. Contracts signed."

He sits back again in his chair.

I glance at Blitz and we share a conspiratorial smile. He leans in and whispers, "I wouldn't anyway. This is your gig. I just want to watch."

"You ready?" Ivana calls. She sounds a little less put out now. Maybe I've calmed down her concern that she is stuck with someone who doesn't know a *plié* from a cartwheel.

I glance at Blitz and walk over to their corner. Dominika holds out her hand in greeting. It's delicate and finely boned. I imagine that her entire skeleton is make of filigree. She's as dainty and poised as a glass figurine.

"Can we get someone on music?" Ivana asks. "We could really use it for this part."

Dmitri jumps up and heads to the corner, where a sound system sits on a shelf. "The confrontation in Act 1, I presume?" he asks.

"Yes," Ivana says. She turns to me. "Most ballets just act this out, but I want the presentation of the spindle to Aurora to be a dance. Aurora will be intrigued, but her ladies-in-waiting will pull her away. Carabosse will entrance her with a dance and, ultimately, get her to prick her finger."

I nod. All this makes sense.

"Start the music," Ivana says.

The sound begins, and Ivana listens. "Not yet, not here. Aurora is doing the dance with her ladies-in-waiting." She moves her hand, staring up at the ceiling. "Okay, hear that dark note there? That's when the audience will first see Carabosse."

She moves with sudden, menacing steps, then as the music goes on, she gets lighter and straighter. "When the brighter line comes in, this is when you will first approach her with the spindle." She pretends to hold an object in her hand.

"Aurora, you will come forward, then back, forward, then back." Ivana makes the movement. "Then dance away like a lark."

We watch her make small leaps, her hands out and open as if she has nothing to fear.

"Then you, Carabosse, will approach, matching her dance with a heavier note, circling her and holding out the spindle."

She immediately changes position, her shoulders slightly forward, but still executing perfect turns.

"That's enough to get a feel for how well the two of you fit as opposites," Ivana says. "Even through Aurora's costume is pink and Carabosse will be cloaked, everything from hand gestures to posture to dance style must indicate good versus evil, light versus dark."

Dmitri stops the music and starts it again.

"Dominika has her steps, so I'll work with yours," Ivana says. "Mirror me. I expect it to be rough. We shall work on technique later."

I turn to stand beside Ivana so I can match her as best as possible. Sweat pops out on my hairline even though I've done things like this before. When I first learned routines with the choreographers of *Dance Blitz*, we went through the same process.

It takes concentration to follow Ivana, keeping

my posture dark, my movements threatening but evocative, and following the steps. I miss most of the turns, but get most of the arm movements. It's only a short bit, perhaps thirty seconds.

"Again," Ivana says. "Try to get the blocking so we can add Aurora."

On the second run-through, I catch a couple of the turns and stay mostly on pace.

"Dominika, bring in your part," Ivana says. She moves away to give Dominika room to interact with me.

I know this is when they will really start to watch. How quickly can I learn? How do our heights, body styles, postures, and acting work together?

This is different from what I've done before because I never had to prove myself on Blitz's show. I had the part. I just needed to perform it as well as I could.

But at least a live audience isn't sending in votes and commentary today. I'm not sure which is worse. Impressing a million people or just one.

Dmitri restores the music. It feels very different to run through the motions with Dominika so close. She's obviously worked on this segment for a while, as her dancing is flawless, down to her expression. I remember that she lost her parents and wonder how she copes. Maybe I'm seeing it now.

I stay somewhat bent, keeping a less-than-perfect

posture during the first attempt to hand over the spindle. But when Dominika spirits away, I straighten to full power, putting more beauty and strength into the moves.

I'm still missing a turn and several movements are way off, but I have the rough positions. When Dmitri shuts off the music this time, he's smiling.

"She's divine," he says. "Did you see how she adjusted, just like Carabosse would do, when Aurora did not believe her the first time? She's a natural."

"Her dancing is immature," Dominika says.

"She just learned the part," Dmitri says.

"If you must cast her, then put her here," Dominika says. "At least in this role, a kind critic will play off her lack of skill as part of the character."

I bite my lip and catch Blitz's eyes in the mirror. His eyebrows are high, and when his gaze meets mine, he makes a horror-scream face.

This make me almost laugh, but I straighten my expression quickly when Evangeline turns sharply to me.

"I want the other girl," Evangeline says. "She is too good for the corps and has ten years of dance."

"Who was that one?" Ivana asks.

"The one with the strange name. Weeza, or something."

No way! My gaze snaps back to Blitz in the mirror. Another horror face.

Dmitri shakes his head. "Give this Weeza a story-book character. Or make her a fairy. If Livia will do, just think of the publicity. I can picture the poster, Dominika in all her beautiful glory, and a sinister image of Livia menacingly behind her. It will be the talk of the Americans."

For some reason, the mention of Weeza makes me want to win this role, despite what I know will be a battle for six months, or at least the months of rehearsals. Weeza has been the voice of my opposition almost as long as I've known Blitz. She's what I have fought against to get where I am.

So I do something I didn't think I'd ever do.

I go full diva.

"We can reach twenty million Twitter followers with that poster," I say, my voice hard. "Live streams of rehearsals. We can make tickets sell out in minutes."

Then I shrug and glance at Alexei. "It's not my money to lose."

I head over to my bag. "Let me know if you decide you want anyone to actually show up for your little ballet."

I pick up my Crocs and bag and don't look back.

Blitz catches up with me right as we walk out the door.

"Now that was some seriously bad-ass dramatic

diva action there!" he says. "Damn, I wish I'd seen you at that negotiation."

He takes my hand to lead me to the car. I don't want to tell him I was a total wuss in the meeting, letting Juliet do all the talking, feeling like an outcast and a sham.

But I'm starting to see what makes people like Blitz get where he is.

You don't let people make you feel small.

You believe in the power of what you can do.

Chapter Fourteen

Blitz and I haven't even made it home when my cell phone rings.

It's Dmitri.

"Don't answer," Blitz says. "Make them stew in it."

I hesitate for a moment, but I'm not quite to the level where Blitz is in these types of negotiations. So I answer.

"This is Livia."

"Carabosse is yours," Dmitri says. "Even Dominika has stars in her eyes. You think we should get bigger venues?"

"I don't know. How big are they now?" My belly quakes. I talked a lot of talk, but I don't know if I have any real pull. Just because *Dance Blitz* fans like sexy numbers on TV doesn't mean they'll buy a ticket to a ballet.

I glance over at Blitz. He raises his eyebrows. I hurriedly put the phone on speaker.

"The venues range from modest theaters with seating for about five hundred to one or two that could hold a little over one thousand," Dmitri says.

Blitz speaks up. "What were your plans for a DVD of the production?"

Dmitri clears his throat. "We didn't have a budget for that. We are operating as a traditional touring ballet."

"I'm willing to front the cost on the production for a cut in the deal," Blitz says. "Have your guys contact my lawyer. We'll draw it up."

"Very well," Dmitri says. "My, my. A recording." He sounds pleased. "I'll speak with Alexei about it."

"Good. Let us know," Blitz says.

"Good day," Dmitri says.

I end the call.

"I hope that wasn't too forward of me," Blitz says. "I sensed you were anxious about feeling responsible for ticket sales. Our people are more the watch-from-home market."

I nod. "I guess I got the part."

"I'll say!" Blitz says. "You've worked hard these past weeks. Your ability to pick up choreography was spot-on. You're becoming a first-rate entertainer in your own right."

He reaches over and takes my hand to lift it to his

lips. "I could not be more pleased for you," he says. "You are amazing."

I want to say it's all because of him, but it isn't true. I studied ballet for two years before I met him. I was driven. Blitz just provided an opportunity. And I wasn't too afraid to take it.

Although I got close.

"I can't wait to see a list of cities," Blitz says. "I know you'll be caught up in rehearsals and all, but hopefully I can at least visit you on each opening night."

"Of course," I say. "They aren't going to lock the ballerinas in a virgin vault."

He laughs. "I'll be interested in hearing about the living arrangements. Maybe you can room with Weeza."

I pull my hand away from him and hit his shoulder. "Now that's just mean."

But she is going to be there. And if Evangeline expressed to her that she wanted her to be Carabosse but then the part went to me, I'd definitely have a formidable enemy on my hands, maybe even one to rival Giselle.

Chapter Fifteen

W ith the last large roles settled, the cast and crew of *Sleeping Beauty* begin booking their travel to the first leg of the journey, a rehearsal space in Chicago.

I have the option of flying with everyone else or meeting them on the first day. And I can stay in their host hotel, or I can find my own accommodations.

Blitz lies on the bed as I start my preliminary packing. I've never been to Chicago. Is it warm? Does it get cold at night in the summer? I look up weather statistics every five minutes.

"You can always buy more things up there," he says.

"In my free time between rehearsals?"

"Right. I can send Shelly to help." He hesitates. "Or I can come."

I sit down next to him. "What do you think? Should I try to be a part of the troupe? Or take the easy way out and just live with you while I do this?"

We've discussed this for days. Now it's time to decide and I can't draw a conclusion. The travel agent needs to let my reservations with the troupe go if I'm not using them.

"You've established a bit of a diva vibe," Blitz says. "But that was only with a few of them. You could start again, be humble. Eat, sleep, and breathe the ballet with them."

I've never gotten to do that. With Blitz, maybe I never will. I'm not sure of our future, but we could get married, have kids. This might be one of the few times in my life I can just...*go*.

"I'll travel with them," I say. "If I can't handle them any longer, we'll stay together someplace close to the studio, but away from the others."

"Brilliant compromise," Blitz says. "I think a few more friends will do you good. It will be hard to make them with man-meat hanging on your shoulder."

He makes me laugh. Man-meat.

I shove all six pairs of toe shoes in the bag. "Don't let me forget to call Mindy. Maybe she can convince her family to drive to the Houston show if I send tickets."

"Have you thought about asking your parents?" he asks. "It's only a few hours from here."

I frown. I can't imagine that they would come. My dad doesn't seem to want to back down from his opinion of me. But maybe Mom and Andy could drive over.

"I'll try," I promise. "I'll send them tickets. And your parents will come, I assume?"

"Of course! I'll bring them for opening night, unless that makes you nervous." Blitz sits up, eyeing the panties that are flying through the room to land in one of the bags.

"I don't think anything will make more nervous than I already will be," I say. "Familiar faces will probably be good."

Blitz makes the call to Dmitri to say I'll be traveling with the group and heads to another part of the house to poke around the website for the tour to gather dates and cities.

I sit among all the bags. I still have a couple days to pull everything together. I just don't want to be in a hurry and miss something important. Not that there is much of anything that couldn't be replaced.

I pull the blue-sprayed toe shoes from my bag. I don't wear this pair anymore. They are too special, too important to wear out. Toe shoes don't last forever. With the amount of dancing I'll be doing, I could go through a pair every day.

I hug these to me, though. I got them from

Danika. My first pair. Then the wardrobe people from *Dance Blitz* sprayed them to match the dress I wore when I rushed the stage to save Blitz from wrecking his career.

They are almost the only thing I still possess from when I lived at home. I walked away with only two outfits, both of which stopped fitting after the stringent workouts on the show, and a ragged backpack.

It's as though my past was erased. Like it didn't exist.

It's worse now. Gabriella is out of reach. I can't go to my old dance academy.

And now, a new city. New people, some of whom are already against me.

I'm cutting loose, a little, if not a lot, from Blitz too.

I've never stood on my own. Reached for my own thing.

It's time.

I tuck the shoes back in the bag. My life is charmed now, and I know it. I have leverage. Money. Options.

But like Dominika, I've had a lot of loss. I wonder why they chose *Sleeping Beauty*, the fragile damsel who has all the plot events happen *to* her, starting with a curse on her birth. She has no control over anything and can't even rescue herself.

I'm glad I'm playing Carabosse. I might not be the beauty or the star, but at least everything I do onstage will play out based on my own actions, for better or for worse.

Chapter Sixteen

The dancers meet at Jenica's to take a van together to the airport. It's all been very organized, which bodes well for the travel between the legs of the tour.

I decide to have Ted drive me to the studio, preferring to say good-bye to Blitz away from all the squealing girls who would undoubtedly steal the moment.

Blitz and I hold on to each other inside the front door, Ted waiting patiently out by the car. "I can be there by bedtime if you need me," Blitz says.

"I know."

My cheek rests on his soft cool T-shirt as he wraps his arms around me. I'm dressed way down myself, the sort of cute workout outfit you don't actually work out in, black and pale purple with everything matching. I bought it at Target. I don't want to flaunt my position in front of the other dancers by dressing expensively or in a showy way. There will be enough resentment as it is.

Blitz kisses me softly, his fingers sliding down the braid that falls across my shoulder. Then he pulls back, his eyes earnest as he looks into mine. "You will be wonderful. Don't let anyone get you down."

I nod. This is what I wanted. To do something for myself. And I'm on my way.

I turn to the door. I'm not carrying a thing. The car is already loaded. I probably should have packed a little more lightly, but my anxiety about what to wear and having the right things means that I have loaded three large suitcases and a carry-on. Oh, well. They can ridicule my excess if they want. It *is* six months.

Blitz stands in the doorway as I head down the walk to where Ted waits by the car. He didn't bring the Ferrari, per my request, and has a simple black Mazda. I don't want to be flashy, and I sit in the front seat so no one will notice I'm being chauffeured.

Blitz waves as we pull away from the house. I feel a sense of panic as we turn the corner and I can't see him anymore. What was I thinking? Six months? He'll find someone else. Girls will throw themselves at him. It will be over!

I press my hand against my chest, trying to slow down my panic.

"You okay, Livia?" Ted asks.

I nod.

"Exciting day," he says.

I stare out the window. I'm leaving another home-town. Putting everything behind me.

It's too much.

My phone buzzes. I pull it from my purse. It's Blitz.

Miss you already.

This makes me smile a little. I should not doubt him. He's been steady through everything. And he's proud of me. If we weather a separation and get back together, then we'll know for sure this is the right thing.

The landscapes slide by, some still green from spring, others already suffering in the Texas heat. Some people prioritize their yards. Others do not. We all pick what is important to us.

When I return, it will be close to Thanksgiving. Dreamcatcher will already be rehearsing the holiday recitals. My throat thickens.

Another buzz. This time it's Mindy.

I think you're gone already! Slowly working on my parents to see if I can get them to go to your ballet! It seems a million years away! Can't wait!

P.S. Preston finally switched workdays. I see him tomorrow!!!!

Now this makes me smile for real. We text excitedly about this for several minutes until Ted says, "We're here."

I look up. The parking lot of Jenica's is a madhouse. A huge bus. Dancers everywhere, surrounded by suitcases and duffel bags.

I've chosen the right clothes, because everyone is in some form of dance wear, leotards covered with shorts or skirts, tennis shoes, flip-flops. I spot Weeza. She's not wearing tights today, but does have a denim jacket with the sleeves cut off over her black leotard and jean shorts.

It's miserably hot as I step out onto the steaming asphalt. Quite a number of the people are fanning themselves with anything they can get their hands on. Folded paper. Magazines.

Ted gets out to unload my bags. I sit another moment in the air-conditioning. I wonder if I would have ever gotten a role like this without Blitz, if I had just worked on it for my own.

Certainly not a world-class ballet like Dominika's. But maybe something small.

I open my door and step out. A couple dancers notice me but don't react other than to observe Ted getting my bags.

I quickly head to the back of the car to lug one out myself, so he can appear to be a friend, not a driver.

There is no sign of Dmitri or Alexei or any of the

people I've met. Probably they are inside and out of the heat.

I snag handles and roll two of my suitcases toward the mass of people. A girl with a clipboard approaches. She's the one who checked us in for auditions. When we get close enough, she says, "Oh! Livia! You can go inside with Dmitri and the others. You have a separate van coming."

Ted arrives with my bags. "Should I load them for you?" he asks.

This gets a few people's attention.

"Oh, hers can go inside the building," the girl says.

"No," I say quickly. "I'd rather ride with the corps." Then hastily add, "If there's room."

"Well, sure," she says. "But wouldn't you rather be with the principals?"

"No," I say. "I'm fine out here."

She shrugs. "Okay. Just hold on to your bags another minute. The driver is pulling some phony baloney about shift times and he won't open the bus to load our stuff yet."

"I can wait and load them for you," Ted says.

"That's okay, I've got it," I tell him. I want him to go!

He gets it, heading back to the car without another word. I sigh with relief.

A burly man wearing black gloves shoves up the door to one of the under-bus bays.

"Finally!" the clipboard girl says and hurries over.

The mass of dancers surges forward, anxious to load up and get out of the heat.

I have too many bags to take them all at once, so I hang back. I might regret letting Ted leave.

I inch forward, dragging the first two bags closer, then going back for the other one. I keep this process going until a male dancer who has pushed his way back out of the crowd notices and comes over.

"Need a hand?" he asks.

"Sure," I say. "I may have overpacked."

He takes two bags and rolls them forward. "Not all of us travel light."

He's the definition of a career ballet dancer, lean and muscled with a fine, chiseled face. Young, too, twenty at best.

We can't quite get to the bus. There's a crush of people trying to shove their bags inside, plus another wave trying to push back out.

I wait with the man, both of us sweating in the unrelenting sun.

"I'm Andrew, by the way," he says, letting go of one of my suitcase handles to extend a hand.

My stomach turns a little as I shake it. "My little brother is named Andy," I say.

"Then you'll remember mine," he says with a jaunty smile.

"I'm Livia," I say. "Thank you for helping."

"I know who you are," he says. "Everyone here does. The TV show star who gets to be the evil fairy. Everyone's excited you are here."

"Really?"

"Sure. Guaranteed publicity. Good ticket sales. The ballet could be extended, and if this new troupe holds together, another production for us. You're a golden ticket."

"Oh!"

This is not what I had expected.

We move forward.

A few of the girls who have already settled their bags come over. One is short, pixie like, with short brown curls. The other is taller with blond hair.

"Andrew!" the curly-haired one says. "You're sitting by me, right?"

"Count on it!" he says.

They hang around for a minute, looking at me with wide eyes until one finally elbows Andrew.

"Oh, right," he says with a laugh. "Carla, Fiona, this is Livia."

"Hi, Livia," says Carla, the one with curls.

"Hey," I say. I feel a little overwhelmed by all the new people. But now that we're loading, the whole demeanor of everyone has changed. Instead of hot and miserable, there's a party atmosphere. Smiles and laughter and high excitement. It's a little like when all the former *Dance Blitz* contestants arrived for the final show.

We finally make it to the bus bays. They are pretty stuffed, so Andrew has to move some things around to fit in my suitcases. The crowd has mostly loaded into the bus, including Carla and Fiona.

I hold on to my small carry-on and thank him for his help.

"No problem," he says. "Let's see what sort of seats are left."

I follow him up the stairs. When we reach the inside of the bus, the air-conditioning is absolute bliss.

"Andrew! Over here!" Carla calls. She's about halfway back.

There are tons of empty seats. Whole rows with nobody in them.

I aim for one when I hear "Livia!"

I look up. It's Fiona, Carla's friend. She's sitting opposite Carla and Andrew.

"Come with us!" she says.

I hesitate, then walk toward them. I certainly didn't expect this to happen. I sit on the aisle next to Fiona. Andrew is just an arm's length away.

One of the girls behind us pops her head up over the seat back. "Okay, Livia, if you are going to ride with the riffraff, you have to DISH about what it's like to be on *Dance Blitz*!"

There's a chorus of YES all around, and suddenly it's like a sleepover when everyone wants to hear your ghost story.

I can do this.

So as the bus finishes loading and the grumpy driver pulls us out of the parking lot, I start to talk about the sets, the makeup people, the cameras, and the mayhem. I answer their questions, which aren't particularly nosy, mostly about how long we had to learn new dances and how we were trained.

And honestly, I have the time of my life.

Chapter Seventeen

I might have been able to get on the corps bus and switch out of first class on the plane, but when we arrive at our hotel in Chicago, I am expected to take my private room on the secure floor with the principals and staff.

I'm sad about this, having made so many new friends during the day. I know I can go rent my own room on the lower floors, but I'm not sure what Dmitri might plan, if there are meetings that will be up here. So for now, I accept that this is my position and sit alone on the bed wondering what is next.

None of us thought to exchange cell phone numbers while we were all sitting together, so I have no way to talk to anyone.

This will be my home for the six weeks of rehearsals, so I start unpacking, trying to fit the most important things in the six small drawers and three feet of closet rod. I should have brought more hangers, as there are only four in there and I have at least ten dresses and two evening gowns. I have no idea where to buy some. Maybe the hotel has more.

I line up the fifteen pairs of shoes on a shelf, realizing that if I continue to hang out with the corps dancers, all this will be unnecessary. But I really have no idea what I'm getting into. And Dmitri might still be taking me to events where I have to look the part.

Once I've done everything I can do, I sit again. My stomach rumbles but I don't know the plans for dinner. I think we're on our own until first rehearsal in the morning.

I've been spoiled. It starts to all rain down as I realize I have no chef here preparing the perfect blend of carbs and protein to keep me going. No smoothies. No assistant.

Man. I've gotten totally dependent on that lifestyle. And there's no kitchen here. I can't cook for myself.

I figure I might as well see what is nearby. Maybe a health food store or an all-natural cafe or deli. I pick up my purse and prepare to head down alone.

The hall is quiet. I wonder where Dmitri and Dominika and the others are. Maybe they've gone to dinner without me, assuming that if I was going to ditch them for the corps, I would continue to do so.

Dang.

I wait for the elevator. When it arrives, an elderly woman gives me a small smile as she exits to the hall.

I get in alone and press the button for the lobby. My body vibrates with jitters. I'm completely unfamiliar with Chicago, but I have Google Maps, and I can always just call a taxi if I get too lost.

The elevator stops on the sixth floor and slides open.

I'm surprised to see Weeza standing there. She's changed into jeans and a denim jacket, ragged on the bottom, the hem cut out.

"Hello, Weeza," I say as she gets on. She gives a little grunt in reply.

She pushes the button, but just as I'm contemplating the awkwardness of a ride down with her, someone shouts, "Hold the elevator!"

And just like that, we're crowded inside, a dozen dancers squeezing into the small space. There's laughter and whoops and "No way am I eating crab cakes" and general arguments about whether it would be unwise to go out clubbing with rehearsals in the morning.

I don't expect to get swept into it, but one of the girls I met on the plane slides her arm around mine and drags me through the lobby and out into the chilly evening.

"Chicago!" somebody shouts, and the others take up the cry.

Then one girl says, "Roxie!"

And just like they had all planned it, like this was a show everyone had rehearsed, they all line up around her, singing, "The name on everybody's lips is gonna be..."

And the whole rest of them shout, "Roxie!"

And it goes on.

I've never seen or heard what they are singing, but it's amazing. I glance around and see Weeza shaking her head and taking off alone down the sidewalk.

The boys pair up with a girl, and the leftover girls link up, and they are doing sultry spontaneous moves. I take a step back, not sure what to do, then I'm grabbed and bent over the arm of someone I can't even see. My vision blurs, but I'm held in a perfect position while everyone once again says, "Roxie!"

Then we're swirled again and I'm passed to another dancer, another girl, and this time I have to hold on to her as she wraps a leg around me and strikes a dramatic pose while the girl sings another line. Then it's another "Roxie!"

This goes on, the couples mixing and switching out. I get to a boy and he immediately takes me into a lift, and there's another "Roxie!"

People have stopped on the street to video us and I guess that's when everyone decides to break up, running down the street and laughing, and I am swept along with it.

We pile into some little cafe with a dozen tiny round tables, all pushed together in a jigsaw puzzle that doesn't quite connect.

And I'm here.

"That was so nuts!" one girl says, and everyone shrieks with laughter and giggles and astonishment.

"We are gonna do this every single night," another says.

I can't remember any of their names. Andrew and Carla and Fiona aren't here.

But everyone knows me. A phone gets passed around with pictures and video of our dance.

"Tag Livia!" someone says.

There's a chorus of YES and I'm shown a phone with me in the air and all the dancers around. So I type in my Twitter handle and it's out into the world.

"Do you think Blitz will retweet it?" someone asks.

"Just ask her!" another voice insists.

I feel the slight separation now, the person who is different from the rest. They turn to look at me. "Sure," I say. "I'll forward it to him." And I take out my phone.

There's another big YES! And high fives. I tell Blitz to go find the tagged photo and how crazy and fun it's been. But then I have to let it go because people are ordering food and talking and finally someone tells me about the Broadway show *Chicago* and that we were singing one of the famous songs from it.

I'm not the only one who hasn't seen it, thankfully, and we go over the words and decide to do the whole thing again after dinner.

When we get our sandwiches and soups and salads, I look around at everyone and think — is this how regular people live?

Then I realize, no, no it's not. We're dancers. Some of the best. And we're about to embark on something big together. So we're high. Exuberant. Unstoppable.

And it's the best feeling in the world.

Chapter Eighteen

W e stay out way later than we should, wandering the streets and jumping on the train that everyone calls the "El."

I only talk to Blitz for a couple minutes before I'm crashing, and he laughs and tells me to get some sleep. He's retweeted my image plus how to see our show, and our spontaneous Chicago number is already causing the ticket sales to go wild for the ballet. People are complaining that New York is sold out. Maybe they could have gotten bigger venues after all.

In what seems like minutes after I hit the pillow, my phone buzzes with the alarm I set to get ready for the first rehearsal. We're having a group breakfast downstairs then walking together to the studio, which is only a few blocks away.

I braid my hair up and slip on a pale blue leotard and skirt. It's Blitz's favorite, and my signature color from the show. I want to feel as comfortable as I can going into what will surely be a nerve-racking day.

My purple Dreamcatcher dance bag on my shoulder and my favorite Crocs on my feet help give me confidence and a feeling of connectedness to my history as I head to the elevator.

Ivana and Evangeline are already walking down the hall a ways ahead of me. They don't notice I've come out of my room.

"So how long do you give the TV diva?" Evangeline asks Ivana.

"Three days," she answers. "And that's only if I'm nice today."

They laugh, and my stomach burns. So this is what they think of me.

"At least we didn't have to suffer through dinner with her," Ivana says.

"You didn't see what they were up to?" Evangeline asks. "It's all over Twitter." She pulls out her phone.

I slow down, looking side to side to see if there is anywhere I can hide. It's a long hall with nothing but hotel room doors. I think about sneaking back into my room. It's just that they might turn around and see me.

So I straighten my back and keep going.

They make it to the elevator, but they are so

engrossed in looking at the phone, I am able to approach unnoticed.

"They're all dancing in the street," Ivana says with a sneer.

Evangeline doesn't respond to that, but I get the sense that maybe she is a little jealous that she wasn't involved.

"Dmitri will no doubt be thrilled with the publicity," Ivana says, pushing the phone away. "He's practically drooling over her."

Then they see me.

"Good morning," I say.

They have the good sense to look at the floor, embarrassed to be caught talking about me.

I stare up at the number above the elevator. This feels like an important moment. The way I handle it sets the tone for how the next few days will go.

"Three days," I say. "That seems like a reasonable bet." I still don't look at them. "Can I put my money on four?"

Ivana and Evangeline glance at each other, color rising in their faces. I can't see their exact expressions, as I'm still focused on the elevator display. Just the redness in their cheeks from the corner of my vision. Serves them right.

Mercifully, the doors open. There's a burst of laughter. Several corps dancers in leotards are inside, including Carla and Fiona.

"It's Livia!" Carla says when she sees me. "We thought it was going down!"

Carla and Fiona embrace me in a hug. "You ready for the first day?" Fiona asks.

"Like it's my last!" I say cheerfully and cut my eyes for a second at Ivana and Evangeline.

The dancers see their bosses and hush their giggles. "Good morning," Carla says. She tucks a loose brown curl behind her ear self-consciously.

Ivana and Evangeline ignore the dancers and step inside, frowning. They are probably annoyed that the so-called riffraff have made it up to the secure floor, albeit accidentally since they were already on it when we called the elevator up.

I stay on the side with the dancers. "You missed the craziness last night," I say to Carla. "We danced the Roxie number from *Chicago* all over town."

"We saw it this morning!" Fiona gushes. "We were so jelly!"

"You have to text us next time something like that happens," Carla says. "What is your number?" She pulls out her phone.

Fiona elbows her. "She's a celebrity. She's not going to just give it out."

I want to say that's not true, but she is probably right that I should be careful.

"Let's do group chat," Carla says. "I'll send you the link via a DM on Twitter."

I nod. That's a good compromise.

"You have to follow me so I can DM you." She lists her Twitter handle.

I pull out my phone to locate her and follow her back. Technically, my official Livia Mays account, the one Carla is using, doesn't follow people. But I do it anyway.

She types frantically while the elevator goes down. We stop on the sixth floor again, more dancers pushing their way inside, laughing.

They don't even notice Ivana and Evangeline in the back, or don't care, as they carry on with loud greetings and excitement all the way down to the lobby.

We flow out of the elevator like clowns coming out of a tiny car, and I follow the group toward a private room where breakfast is supposedly set up.

"Are all our meals going to be like this?" Fiona asks as we stand in line for a buffet. Dmitri greets everyone by the door, shaking hands and smiling.

"Beats me," Carla says, bent over her phone. She elbows me. "Invite sent."

I'll look at it later. I notice Ivana and Evangeline peeling off in a different direction. They must have their own breakfast area.

Dmitri sees me and points down the hall.

I shake my head, so he simply says, "Good morning. Eat well! It's a long time until lunch."

"Will we do this every morning?" Fiona asks.

"Monday through Friday," Dmitri says. "We'll distribute schedules here and make sure everyone knows where to go. You have lunch and dinner on your own."

"Cool," Carla says.

We make our way inside the room.

The girl who checked us in during auditions asks our names and hands us a printed schedule. Carla and Fiona are corps dancers and have the same hours.

"I don't have yours," the girl says.

I nod. I figure mine is in some other room, wherever Dmitri was trying to get me to go.

We're handed a cup of Greek yogurt and a plate of fruit, then a slice of ham and scrambled egg whites. A girl at the end asks if we would like a piece of toast.

"I'm going to be starving by lunch," Andrew says behind us. We turn to see him about three people back.

"Time to find a Micky D's," Carla says.

This makes me think of Blitz.

"I would never pollute my body with that trash," Andrew says in front of the woman handing him a double portion of egg whites.

But when we're past the serving table, he whispers, "Please tell me there is fast food within walking distance."

The girls laugh and the four of us sit together at a round table. We're joined by two more girls I remember from last night.

I make sure I eat. I'm feeling better about my ability to manage the storm that will surely rain down when I'm alone with Ivana or Evangeline. I have friends already. No doubt if those two are cruel to me, they will be tough on the others too. We can commiserate together.

The clipboard girl comes up to our table and hands me a half sheet of paper. "Your schedule," she says, then takes off.

Carla turns it around so she can see it. "Oh, wow, you're already working with Dominika today," she says. "We just have random trainers."

"I had to practice with her back in San Antonio," I tell them. "They wanted to make sure I would be a good Carabosse to her Aurora."

"You're the evil fairy?" one of the girls asks. "That is awesome."

"It's what I asked for," I say, then realize it's the wrong thing when the others stop eating.

"You didn't audition?" Carla asks.

"Yes and no," I say, my face hot. "Dmitri wanted to bring me on. I had to pass a rehearsal with Dominika, Ivana, and Evangeline."

"That must have sucked," Fiona says. "One of my

friends is a fairy, and she says the choreographer is a total bitch."

I'm not sure what to say exactly. "It wasn't easy," I say. "I almost walked out."

This placates them. "You'll have to dish later," Carla says. She glances at the clock. "Time to get out of here."

We scarf the rest of our breakfast and quickly follow the other dancers out the door.

The morning is cool, so different from the San Antonio summer days that start hot and stay hot.

"It feels great out here!" Andrew says. "SO glad to be out of Texas."

The girls dig jackets out of their bags. I've tied mine around my waist but take it off to wear properly.

The studio is immense. We enter a foyer with a towering ceiling and fancy glass sculptures of ballerinas hanging by wire. There are hallways in three directions. Everyone consults their schedules.

"I'm that way," Andrew says, pointing off to the left.

"We're the opposite," Carla and Fiona say.

"Do we all have lunch at twelve-thirty?" I ask.

"I do," Andrew says.

"We're eleven-thirty," Carla says with a pout.

"I'll join the group chat," I say. "We'll catch up."

"Group chat?" Andrew asks.

"Check your Twitter," Carla says. "We gotta go!"

Dancers peel off in all directions. I review my own schedule and glance up at the sign that lists the studio rooms. I'm straight ahead.

My hall is quiet. The walls are almost all solid windows looking into dance spaces, some small, others larger. Dancers are assembling in most of them. I keep going until I am near the end of the corridor.

A friendly-looking man is inside. He is not in dance gear, but cargo pants and a T-shirt. He has sandy hair and looks to be a little older than Blitz.

"Livia?" he asks when I open the door.

"Yes," I say.

He extends a hand. "I'm Franco, the acting coach."

"Oh!"

He laughs. "I work with all the roles who will have to convey the story through gestures and expressions."

This is unexpected.

"I expect you had coaches like me on the TV show," he says.

"Not really," I say. "We were mostly told to be ourselves. But I did have a dance teacher who tried to help me get my sexy on."

Franco laughs. "Was that hard?"

"With thirty cast and crew watching me crawl across the floor? Yes!"

He laughs again. "Well, today you get to be the bad guy."

We work on posture and framing and remembering to stay positioned toward the audience, even when a character is beside you. We laugh a lot, and when our session is over and it's time for me to move on, I look forward to meeting with him again later in the week.

For a first morning that started out sort of sketchy, it's shaping up to be a good day.

But as I glance at my schedule to see where I go next, I see what Carla did when she read my page at breakfast. Next up: Dominika.

Chapter Nineteen

M y happy vibes from working with Franco quickly disappear as I head down the hall to where Dominika will be waiting for me.

I want to make a quick call to Blitz and get a little boost, but there isn't time and all the studios can see perfectly into the hall. I don't want to look like some cell phone diva as I approach.

So I straighten my spine and steel myself as I come in range of Studio 12.

I'm surprised when I get there to see Dominika warming up alone.

I push open the glass door.

"Hello," she says pleasantly before moving deeper into a stretch. "I'm not prepped yet."

"Me neither," I say, setting down my bag. "I was with Franco getting my evil fairy on."

She looks at me curiously. "What does this mean, 'getting my evil fairy on'? Did you wear a costume?"

I forget sometimes she is Russian. Her English sounds good. "It's an expression. It's like putting on a personality."

She nods and her tiny arched brows knit together as she considers this oddity.

I kick off my Crocs and sit on a bench to slide on my toe shoes.

"Is Ivana coming to this rehearsal?" I ask.

"I don't think so. She is working with the Prince this morning," Dominika says.

I stand up and do a few hops to get my muscles warm. Dominika is like an ice princess in a white leotard and tights. Her hair is a blond color so close to ash as to almost match her outfit, especially in the harsh overhead light.

She is bony, her muscles stretched taught over her birdlike frame. When she bends over, it seems perfectly possible that she can fold up into a tiny package that would fit in the shoe cubbies.

She could make anyone feel fleshy, and I grimace at the lack of definition in my thighs as I reach for the floor. True career ballerinas have blocks of visible leg muscles. Even though no one would ever call me overweight by any measure, it's clear I haven't done enough dance to burn away all the fat.

Six weeks of ten-hour rehearsals on yogurt and

egg whites will probably do it, though. I think back to how I looked before the three months with *Dance Blitz* and realize I have yet another metamorphosis ahead. I wonder if my parents will even recognize me if they come to the ballet. I don't look anything like the girl I once was.

I don't feel like her either.

After a few minutes, a woman I've never met enters the studio. "Sorry to be late," she says. "The fairies ran over." She drops a bag on the floor and takes her phone over to the sound system.

I want to ask Dominika who this person is, but judging by the confused tilt of her head, I'm guessing she's never seen her before either.

The woman turns around. "I'm sorry we did not get a chance to meet before. I'm Teresa, one of the dance coaches. I work at this studio year-round. I'll be with you until you go on tour, working on technique."

Dominika stands a little straighter, as if suggesting that her technique needs work is an insult.

Teresa notices the prima ballerina's stiff stance and smiles. "Do not worry, Dominika," she says. "I'm not here to change you. I just want to make sure you and Livia look very opposite other than in a few key places where Ivana wants you to almost dance in tandem."

I will have to try and match Dominika's style? I

hope it's for only very brief moments because I can't even imagine getting anywhere near her poise and perfection.

"Come, ladies," Teresa says. "Since the pianists are all otherwise occupied, I've created a loop of the scene where Carabosse gives Aurora the spindle. I understand you've had an introduction to the choreography already."

My face burns. That was two weeks ago and I haven't practiced it since, afraid I would get it wrong and have to break a bad habit.

But Dominika nods. When the music moves into the section with the spindle, she moves effortlessly into the dance.

I can't remember a thing. I watch, painfully, as Dominika dances alone. I have some vague ideas of where I should stand, and I recognize one part where we are moving back and forth as if we are on opposite ends of a teeter-totter.

But mostly I just stand there looking rather stupid.

"I've only learned the critical parts," Teresa says with a frown. "But we'll work on those." She waits for the music to fade out, then back in at the beginning.

She places me facing Dominika and I remember to hold the pretend spindle, at least. When I lift it to her, she turns away in an elegant pirouette that alternates between bent leg and extended.

"Here is where you mimic her," Teresa says.

I do a similar pirouette, sensing my clumsiness compared to Dominika.

"That's it," Teresa says. "Then quicker and closer together until you are doing it at the same time."

I continue the pirouette sequence, sensing we are way off.

"The timing will come," Teresa says. "Let's work on legs and arms and hands. Dominika, since Livia will be holding a prop, we'll have to adjust your arm so that you can match her anyway."

Dominika nods. Teresa stands us side by side, tucking my elbow in, hand near my ribs as if I am holding something, then having Dominika approximate the position.

We review the precise timing of the pirouettes, dancing them over and over again until I start to lose my ability to avoid feeling dizzy, and one of the spins knocks me off balance.

I put my foot down early and miss the next element of the pirouette.

Teresa stops the music.

"It's all right," Teresa says. "That many turns in two hours would get to anyone."

Two hours? I check the overhead clock and see that it is after noon.

"Let's go ahead and break," Teresa says. "I'll see you two again tomorrow. You'll have reviewed choreography by then and should be able to put together more of this scene."

My steps aren't completely steady as I head for my bag. Too little breakfast. Too many turns. Nerves on edge. And it's only the first half of the first day.

It's not quite the lunch hour yet when I walk out into the open foyer. I examine the hanging glass sculptures, wondering if I will find Andrew for lunch or have to figure things out on my own.

Then I remember the group chat.

I open Twitter to see what the link is.

My notifications are outrageous, but I'd expect that after Blitz retweeted that dance image.

But there's another image getting tagged with my Twitter handle.

I pull it up and let out a sigh. Seriously?

It's an obvious Photoshop fake of Blitz with Giselle. They are gazing at each other fondly in front of the *Dancing with the Stars* logo. The Tweet says they will be working together on the show.

Her hair isn't cut out well and the colors from the light on their shoulders don't even match the neon of the sign. But people are buying it, some angry that he's already cheating on me, others excited that he's dancing on TV again.

Uggh. I move on to my direct messages. Sure enough, Carla has sent me a link to download some chat app. I look around. I must be early, as no one else is coming out of the studios yet.

There's a crystal bench in the middle of the foyer, so I sit on it to download the app and accept the invitation to join the private group. So far, the only people in it are Carla, Fiona, Andrew, and now me.

Andrew messaged between his rehearsals to say we could meet in the foyer for lunch.

I glance at the time. Still five minutes.

A few girls come out finally, laughing and happy as they cross the foyer and go out the doors. They don't even look my way.

Then more. Several of these were on the bus and wave at me, but they have places to be and hurry out as well.

I feel very much alone and obvious out on the bench. I want to move to the side wall, someplace less conspicuous. All my old insecurities rear up. I'm too strange, too old-fashioned, too out of touch with regular people.

Maybe I'm not going to make four days after all. Or the three Ivana and Evangeline were giving me.

Perhaps these more experienced people see me more clearly than I see myself.

Then it all turns around.

Andrew comes out, along with two other female dancers. He waves me over, and I'm brought along with this happy crew to eat veggie burgers at a cafe down the street.

The reversals are so swift. I'm like a pendulum, shifting from anxiety to acceptance. Without Blitz, I have no ballast to keep me even and steady. I will have to figure out how to do this on my own.

It will be okay. I must be patient. And I must have faith.

Chapter Twenty

The next few weeks are a blur.

There are trainers I like, including Teresa and Franco.

There are moments that are hard, usually those involving Ivana and Evangeline.

My scenes with Dominika are not the most difficult for her by far, so after a few days of practice, I see her very little. She has many much more technical scenes with fairies and the Prince and her solos.

I spend a lot of time with the artistic director, an older lady named Barb who danced for the New York City Ballet for decades. She's funny and warm, but very exacting. I probably would have liked her if she wasn't sharply criticizing my dance four hours a day.

Much of the time I'm with Barb and the fairies, learning the opening scene where I place a curse on the baby princess. It's a long scene with many parts, and tons of cast members come in and out, from the king and queen to the nurse and baby, fairies and corps dancers male and female. It's crazy and only one of the studios is large enough to hold us all.

Dancers line the walls, sitting on the floor when it's not their turn to come in. A funny young man in a newsboy cap plays the piano in the corner. Sometimes when we blow a scene or Barb stops us in irritation, he'll play a silly line to go along with her mood. A villain's entrance. The theme to *Jaws*.

Barb often cuts him annoyed looks, but he's impervious to her disapproval.

The only breaks in the day are lunch, costume fittings, and physical therapy to make sure we are not stressing our bones or joints. I dance less than many of the ballerinas. The corps dancers are particularly stressed. Carla and Fiona and Andrew are constantly complaining about fatigue.

Blitz and I talk via FaceTime every night. He's filling his days with the two male gymnasts at Jenica's. He is pretty sure between the aerial silks and the trampoline acrobatics he's learning, he could run away with a circus.

"I'm willing to work for peanuts," he says, kicked back on our sofa.

I look greedily at him, at the house behind him. It all feels so far away.

"I'm not sure a ballerina can support your life-style," I say.

"Oh, you didn't see the cut I just made for you on the DVD," he says. "You're on the cover, you're a costar. Forget that no-name Prince. He doesn't even show up for half of it."

I shake my head. Blitz is good to have on my side.

I miss him, but my exhaustion is so complete that I think about it a lot less than I expected. My friendships with Carla, Fiona, and Andrew are helpful in the scenes where we are together. It's nice to have someone to sit by and chat with when I'm not dancing.

I haven't seen Weeza the entire time we've been here, other than glimpses at breakfast. She's obviously not a corps dancer, or she would be in the curse scene with the rest of us. Evangeline must have moved her up to a role in Act 3, the wedding. I'm not in that one at all, so it makes sense we haven't crossed paths.

During the fourth week, a new girl arrives in rehearsals and introduces herself to me. She says she is my understudy, and she will be doing my role during some rehearsals in case I can't perform.

More understudies appear in the next few days, including one for Dominika and the Prince.

I finally see Weeza during costume fittings about two weeks before opening night. The head seamstress is fitting a piece of fur to her bodice. She must be White Cat.

I bite back a giggle at the thought of the girl who always wears black suddenly going out in white. She spots me and carefully looks away. It's strange that she has some grudge against me, even now. I guess she lumps me in the sellouts and is even more incensed that I got the part she wanted for herself.

Still, I try to talk to her.

"I've heard White Cat is a really fun role," I say.

She shrugs. "It's short."

"Something you can build on for the next opportunity," I say, remembering what Juliet told me.

Weeza shrugs again, so I give up on having a conversation.

My costume is glorious. Black and glittery, it's a short traditional tutu covered in a long flowing overdress. For the opening scene, I wear it all, large and imposing and dark as night. Then, when I disguise myself as a peasant to present the hidden spindle to Aurora, I wear a light-colored cape over only the smaller tutu, to allow for our push-pull of a dance.

Once she's been pricked, my minions bring me the overdress again, so I'm back to my full presence of sparkling black.

I do have a bit of a bone to pick with the way the waking-up scene plays out. In all the *Sleeping Beauty* stories I've seen, Carabosse is a force to be reckoned with, a dragon or a powerful enchantress.

In the ballet, they kind of cut to the chase. I stand guard over Aurora with my minions, but when the Prince arrives, the Lilac Fairy sort of waves her hands around, and I'm defeated.

Just like that.

Hollywood would never stand for such an anticlimax.

But this is classical ballet, and so when Angelique uses her paltry magic that couldn't even break my terrible spell, I collapse to be carried out by the crow-like minions.

Being a villain isn't all it's cracked up to be. At least not in the end.

As we approach the dress rehearsals and opening night, the intensity of the workout schedule definitely drops a notch. I guess they don't want anyone injured right at the end. The understudies are working harder than we are.

I watch mine dance with Dominika in the spindle scene and admit to feeling some chagrin. She's better than me by a long shot. She should probably have the role.

But the publicity for the tour is in full swing and I'm definitely a headliner. It's nothing like a TV show. There's no photographers stalking us or interviews. But I do end up on a Chicago station morning show and Dominika doesn't. She never mentions it, but I feel the coolness of both her and the dancer playing the Prince in the final rehearsals.

Blitz takes care of sending tickets to Mindy and her family, since they probably shouldn't come from me. He makes it look like they won them and includes a night stay in a hotel in case they can't afford one.

I hold on to a set I plan to send to my parents. The Houston part of the tour is still many weeks away. We start here in Chicago, then move on to Boston, Baltimore, New York, and Miami. After Houston, there will still be Los Angeles and Seattle.

I've never been to most of these places, only LA. I hope we have time to see the cities. Blitz is coming along on the entire tour, and I've decided to break away from the company at that point to stay in places where we can ensure our security plus have our driver and support staff so I can have a little more freedom.

He and his parents will arrive the night before we open in Chicago. I can't wait to see him. I know I look different, as I expected. More angular, muscular, and strong. I move like a ballerina all the time now, not just when I'm dancing. I've made a metamorphosis, like a butterfly from a cocoon.

I'm who I was always supposed to be.

Chapter Twenty-One

Blitz arrives in Chicago the day before opening night. I want to go pick him up from the airport, but I'm stuck in final rehearsals and fittings.

I remember Juliet telling me that ballerinas do their own makeup, and it turns out it is true, even in big productions like this one. I frantically call around and secure a makeup artist who can travel with me. It will cost a good chunk of money from my *Dance Blitz* days, but it's worth it not to have to worry about some reviewer saying I look ridiculous, or worse, having it sweat into rivulets partway through a dance.

Dominika hears about what I've done and asks if we can split the cost and share her. I'm glad to do so, both for the money savings and in hopes we can bridge the divide between us over the publicity.

The day finally ends well past dinnertime. I hurry

out of the studio, frantically texting Blitz to see where he might be.

When I get to the hotel, there's a party or something going on in the bar to the left of the lobby. The noise is tremendous. I'm wondering if it's something to do with the ballet, when some girl cries out, "I love you, Blitz Craven!"

Of course.

I try to make my way through the melee, but it's a mob. I spot Blitz's parents sitting off to one side in a booth and head for them instead.

David stands when he sees me. "Your boy is trapped," he says. "You might want to go save him."

"Let him save his own wretched self," Renata says, reaching her arms out for a hug.

I lean in for a quick squeeze and drop my dance bag in the booth.

"This could go on for hours if he doesn't have a bodyguard," I say.

"We didn't bring anyone," Renata says. "We flew here with him."

I let out a long sigh. I had forgotten what this is like. Apparently so did Blitz.

I spot an empty chair at the end of the bar. The mob is at the center of the long wooden counter.

Okay, I can work with this.

I slip off my Crocs and leave them by the booth. I have dance slippers on underneath. I take a small bouncing run to the chair, leap onto the seat, then up onto the bar.

My movements catch the attention of the bartender, then the edges of the crowd. I leap over tip jars and empty glasses until I'm in the center of the mob. As I expected, Blitz is trapped by it, pressed against the bar.

I hold out a hand to him.

He looks up. "I never thought I'd be rescued by a ballerina," he says.

"Won't be the last time," I say.

He hops up on a chair, then he's beside me, standing on the bar.

Cheers erupt from down below as he kisses me. There are cell phone flashes and the general lighting of the place increases as all the screens flicker on to video us.

Blitz picks me up and turns us in a circle on the bar. The whoops grow louder.

"You are light as a feather," he says. "Don't they feed the dancers around here?"

"Ten hours of dancing a day," I say. "And no McDonalds in sight."

"We'll have to fix that," he says. "The first burger is on me."

He starts walking along the bar. The crowd tries to move with us, but I see a couple hotel employees with gold badges trying to shift them toward the door.

Blitz steps down on the last chair, gripping me tightly as we hop to the ground. The crowd is kept at bay as we escape to the far side of the bar.

We circle the long way back around to his parents' booth. Most of the fans have been escorted out.

David scoots over to make room for us. "About time they kicked those kids out," he grumbles. "A man can't have a decent drink without getting mobbed."

He frowns into his beer and takes a drink.

"Thank you for fetching him, Livia," Renata says. Her hair is piled elegantly on her head and her black linen jacket looks new.

David is the same as always, in a loose navy *guayabera* with elaborate stitching. His hair is combed over, curling on the ends over his ear. He looks like a curmudgeonly grandfather.

A waitress stops by to ask for our drink order. I just get water. "Big day tomorrow," I say. "The last thing I need is a hangover."

Renata nods. "Sensible," she says.

"So what happened?" I ask Blitz. "Did somebody out you?"

"Right off the bat," he says. "We checked in, got on the secure floor, and came down for a drink. At first it was just a couple girls, but then they texted people, and it snowballed."

"You just need to be a little more forceful with them," David says. "Show them who's boss."

"It was fine," Renata says. "Just unexpected. How are you, Livia? You look so different!"

"Grateful not to be injured," I say. "It was a lot more workout than I'm used to."

"I'll say," Blitz says. He keeps squeezing parts of me, my arms, my shoulders, my waist. "You're all muscle."

"She was already damn skinny," David says.

"It's just a few months," I say. "I'm sure I'll be back to my old self by Christmas."

"You think you'll keep doing ballet work?" Renata asks.

I glance at Blitz. "I'm just taking it one job at a time right now."

The bar quiets down. It almost feels as if no time has passed, and I've just walked up to meet Blitz and his parents in San Antonio.

Except. Well, some parts of me are waking up just being next to him. I think about how it's been six weeks and I'm dying now that he's here.

Blitz is probably in a similar frame of mind because he scoots out of the booth and takes my hand.

"If you'll excuse us, I'm sure Livia is tired and

would love to get some rest before her big opening night tomorrow," he says.

David coughs into his hand. "Some rest. Sure," he says with a laugh.

Renata taps his arm to make him stop. "Sounds perfect. We'll see you tomorrow after the show, dear."

Blitz scoops up my dance bag and my forgotten shoes. He drops his sunglasses on his face despite the darkness of the bar and we stroll out to the lobby.

The elevator doors have barely closed when he's on me, pulling me against his chest. "I'm going to kiss every inch of these new muscles of yours," he says.

I'm still fairly warm and limber from a day of rehearsal, so when he reaches down for my thigh, I can raise my leg straight up to rest on his shoulder.

"Oh man, oh man, oh man," Blitz says, turning to bite my ankle through the stretchy leg warmer.

We're in this position when the doors open on the sixth floor. I notice the number and know it's where all the dancers are staying. But I can't get my leg down before Weeza steps in.

Then backs out. "Forget it," she says.

I wonder why she's going up rather than down, unless she's planning to visit Evangeline. But she doesn't have a card that allows her on the secure floor.

She keeps backing away until finally the doors close again.

I put her from my mind and turn back to Blitz. "You were saying?"

He shifts and sweeps my other leg off the floor. He settles me against his chest, my dance bag banging his shoulder and my shoes dangling from his fingers beneath my back.

"You are going to be naked before the door is closed," he says.

"Oh, really?" I say. "Will you at least let me shower first? I've been dancing since nine this morning!"

"In the shower, then," he says. The elevator door opens on our floor, and he takes off down the hall. I spot the same elderly lady as on the first day and her eyes grow wide as she watches me being carried by Blitz.

I bury my face in his shoulder, stifling a laugh, as we hurry past the other doorways. I could run into anyone up here. Ivana. Evangeline. Dmitri. We might be staying next to one of them! They will hear!

But we continue through another set of doors that require a key card. Then more doors. I'm guessing they aren't in here. At least not Ivana and Evangeline.

We're safe.

Blitz shoves the card key in the reader and shoulders open the door.

When we're inside, he tosses me on the bed. I let

out a little shriek as I go airborne and he dumps my shoes and bag on the floor.

"That leotard is coming OFF," he says, tugging on one of the wine-colored leg warmers.

He peels them down and tosses them across the room. I can barely take in the place, large and spacious but not quite a suite.

He assesses the rest of my outfit and goes for the skirt first, sliding it down and throwing it behind him in a puff of netting.

Then he grasps the top of the leotard to start peeling layers away.

The air hits my skin, chest, ribs.

Blitz lifts my hips to get it down to my knees, then it's flying across the room.

"Always the tights," he mumbles, grasping the waistband and pulling.

"Got to make it a challenge," I say.

"Oh, you're a challenge," he retorts.

When I'm naked on the bed, he kicks off his loafers and pulls his shirt over his head. He starts to take off his pants, but then sort of dives forward, his mouth landing on a breast.

I arch up to meet him, reveling in the feel of him, finally. I'd shut those thoughts out for the most part, not wanting to get too lonely or too homesick for him.

But now it's back, all of it, every memory, every

need. My desire for him blasts through me like a shock wave. I feel consumed, covered in fire.

"Shower, please," I manage to say.

He doesn't move his lips from their soft surround against my tender skin. But he shifts me down so I'm closer to the edge of the bed. Then he's able to slide off and get to the snap of his jeans.

His pants hit the floor, then his boxers.

He lifts me up, wrapping my legs around him so we walk together to the bathroom.

"This is going to kill me," he says, shoving the glass door aside and reaching in to turn on the spray.

Thankfully the water is hot almost immediately. It's a broad standing shower, so Blitz sets me down ahead of him and enters behind me, pulling the door closed.

The small space steams up quickly. I relax into the spray as I let down my hair, relieved to feel the sweat and stickiness of the day washing away.

Blitz tugs a washcloth from the rack on the wall and wets it. "I am going to make sure every inch of you is clean."

He squeezes green body gel from a tiny bottle onto the cloth and works it until it suds up.

"I'm going to start here," he says, bending down to slide it around my ankles. "I want to look at these legs."

The soap makes my skin slippery, and his fingers

glide along, feeling every curve and ridge. I haven't quite gotten the boxy thighs of longtime ballerinas, but the muscles are defined and firm.

He makes his way up, the cloth coming around and behind until he squeezes the new version of my butt.

"Jesus," he says. "It's perfectly smooth."

His face is near my belly button, and one hand slides up my abs, a finger slipping beneath my ribs. "We both have a six-pack," he says. "We should do a photo shoot."

I huff out a quick laugh, trying to imagine posing that close to naked. "I don't think that's my speed," I say.

"I probably would have to buy all the copies so no one else would see anyway," he says. "I'm the jealous sort."

"Are you?" I tease. "The sort to punch somebody for saying I'm a 'sick ride'?"

His laugh is low and rumbly. "My misspent youth."

Water drips off my body and onto his head.

"Less talking, more action," I tell him. "It's been way too long."

"You don't have to tell me twice," he says. He drops the washcloth, most of the gel washed out, and runs both his hands over my skin, back, waist, hips. He's still kneeling.

Then he lifts one of my thighs to his shoulder. He cradles me with his arms as his lips slide down my belly, his tongue finding its way.

I press my hand against the tile for balance, my breath catching. The water cascades down my back as he works, warm and relaxing.

He's back. He's here. He's mine.

The spiraling starts small and tight, just where he's working my body. Then it begins to spread, a warmth that circles out like a pebble dropped in a river.

He adds fingers, and everything starts to speed up. I find the handle to the shower door and grip it tight. God, I've missed this. The tension. The anticipation. The pleasure. The tension gathers quickly now and I'm almost over the edge.

Then the rhythm begins, pulsing against Blitz's mouth. I let it take me over, bliss washing over me in its wake. My tears mix with the shower water. I'm overcome with happiness and relief. The time apart hasn't mattered. This is real.

Blitz lowers my leg but keeps his hold on me. I'm glad, as my muscles are shaking. He shuts off the water and pushes open the door to fetch a towel.

"To be continued in the bedroom," he says. "I might not let you sleep, but I'll let you rest."

He stands over me, tall, solid, my Blitz. He wraps me in the towel, squeezing my hair.

We walk together to the bed, crisp and white, and when I lay down on it, it's cool to the touch.

Blitz pulls the towel away and smooths my hair back. "I want a better look," he says.

He glides his fingers along my shoulders, following the curve of those muscles. Then between my breasts, where my chest is tight and flat between them. And back to my legs, which he still can't get enough of, lifting one to kiss the entire length.

"Amazing," he says. "I bet you can jump *grand jetés* over my head."

"I'm not sure about that," I say. "But I won't apologize for my form anymore."

During the weeks of rehearsals, we've talked about Barb and Franco and all the instructors. He knows how hard it's been. Now is for reunion, reconnection.

And Blitz takes his time. Kissing, kneading, touching. I know the night will go late, but as he promises, I am at rest, and he worships me.

Chapter Twenty-Two

I wish I could take Blitz with me for every part of the process leading up to opening night, but the way he's mobbed yet again as soon as he gets out on the sidewalk outside the hotel, I know it's unwise.

"They're just going to wait for you out here," I say as we duck back inside. "I'll ride with the troupe over to the theater."

"I should spend the day with my parents anyway," he says. "They're lost in new cities."

"I'll see you after the show," I say. "I think there's an after-party." I actually know for a fact that there is, but I'm not entirely sure I want to go. Blitz stealing Dominika's big night with fans and paparazzi would not help us work better together.

He presses a kiss to my forehead. "Don't miss the bus. I'll see you tonight."

We part reluctantly and I load up with the rest of the dancers.

Our last week has been entirely at the venue as the crew worked in the lights and scenery and we practiced our entrances and exits. The feel of each dance is different in the expansive space of the stage without a barre or mirrors or glass walls.

I thought I was accustomed to the glamour and beauty of lights and stage and how a final number comes together. But a classical ballet is a completely different animal from a TV show. The live orchestra makes it magical. And the lack of cameras and screens helps preserve the illusion that we have stepped into a medieval world.

I think Blitz will be dazzled by it. We're recording the DVD version in New York, which gives us time to get everything perfect. We have the most shows there plus time for the crew to come in and film a rehearsal so they aren't obtrusive to the audience.

The atmosphere on the bus is absolutely giddy with excitement. Every time someone reaches the top step to become visible to those already seated, a great "Huzzah!" rises up.

When I reach the position, the cries reach a fever pitch. Some of the dancers chant, "Carabosse! Carabosse!" So I hunker down to give them my best evil hunchback look.

Everyone erupts in cheers and laughter. I sit by

Carla, opposite Andrew and Fiona. It's hard to imagine that our first show is already tonight.

"This is the beginning of the end, you know," Carla says, tucking her curls into her bun. It's a futile gesture, as every time she gets one put away, another escapes.

"It is," agrees Andrew. "Once we're past opening night, it will be a blur of travel and stages and shows."

The last few dancers load on and the driver closes the door. The girl with the clipboard, who I finally learned is named Penny, stands to look over us and make sure everyone is here.

I glance out the window to see Dominika, Dmitri, Evangeline, Ivana, Barb, and the Prince loading into a limo. I'm glad I'm not traveling with them, imagining the serious, grim-faced ride.

"Where is Weeza?" Penny says, leaning down to look out the window.

I glance over at Carla and raise my eyebrows. The three of them know I have a history with her, but not that Evangeline wanted Weeza to play Carabosse. I'm glad she got White Cat, though, and did not end up being my understudy. I'm quite sure she would have broken my kneecaps to get the role.

The driver opens the door again as Penny turns and heads down the steps. She goes into the hotel, furiously tapping on her phone.

But when she comes out, Weeza behind her,

Weeza has her arm wrapped around Angelique, the girl playing the Lilac Fairy. Instead of coming up to the bus, they head toward the limo.

Fine by me.

Carla looks out and watches them load in. "I wonder why she's moved up."

"Sex," Andrew says. "She's been all over Angelique since week three."

Oh! That possibility hadn't even occurred to me.

"We can take a limo over tomorrow if you want," I say. "Blitz has one hired for his whole stay."

"Are we trading a limo for sex too?" Andrew asks.

"Sex not necessary," I tell him with a laugh.

"Oh! A limo!" Fiona says excitedly. "Can we take it to the party tonight too?"

I frown. I'm not sure I'm going. "I have to do the meet-and-greet event with the patrons," I say. "I might be done for after that."

"Nonsense," Carla says. "We will all be high as kites and ready to go out all night."

Penny gets back on the bus and the driver shifts us out of the circle and out onto the street. We've been having to get ourselves over to the theater all week and mostly took the El, speeding through town on the train. But on show days, they want us to go together and be accounted for. Still, I'm sure I could get the limo cleared for us if I wanted.

Why not have a little fun?

"You guys could take the limo while I'm stuck at the patron event," I say.

"Yes! A pink one," Andrew says. "With white carpet."

"Andrew, you are too much," Fiona says. "I want it to have a hot tub inside."

I laugh and shake my head. "Do they even make those?"

"Heck yeah," Andrew says. "I saw it on some TV show about the rich and famous."

We speed through the streets. It's morning, but past rush hour. I wonder what Blitz will do with his parents all day, but mostly I try to figure out if it's a good idea to go to the party. Especially in a hot tub limo.

Still, I text a quick note to Blitz making sure whatever he got for tonight will have enough room for three more.

Any special requests? Blitz texts back.

I mention pink with white carpet or hot tub.

Blitz's next text is nothing but exclamation marks and other random characters.

Carla looks over my shoulder. "Is that Blitz?" she asks.

"It is," I say.

"So wild." Her eyes meet mine. "Famous people, sitting right beside me."

"She's been with you for six weeks," Andrew says. "You should be over it by now."

"Blitz is new," she says. "And I may or may not have a picture of him on the wall of my apartment."

"Eeeuuuwww," Fiona says. "You have to take that down. You can't have Livia's boyfriend on your wall with your kissy kisses all over it."

Carla tosses her empty water bottle at her. "There are no kissy kisses!" She glances at me. "At least, they shouldn't be noticeable."

I shake my head. I guess I haven't really been out in the normal world with friends I would talk with like this since Blitz. Everyone in my life in San Antonio was respectful of my relationship with him, like the Dreamcatcher teachers and everyone at Jenica's.

I forget that a significant chunk of the young female population probably has a crush on him.

"So, do we get to meet him proper?" Andrew asks. "Is he coming to the party?"

I'm not sure how to answer that. "I'm not sure if he should go," I admit. "I think he might overshadow all the hardworking dancers. He wouldn't like that."

"She has a point," Carla says. "Maybe we should all just blow off the party."

"It's opening night!" Fiona exclaims.

Andrew holds up his hands. "I say we go to the

party until Livia arrives." He turns to me. "You simply have to come for a while."

I think about this. "I don't think the meet and greet is very long. So maybe."

"It's all settled!" Carla says, sitting back. "This is going to be an epic day."

I have to agree with her about that.

Chapter Twenty-Three

The final fittings and rehearsals go perfectly. I may not match Dominika's style as perfectly as Ivana may have wanted in the spindle scene, but it's passing to everyone else. Maybe pleasing Ivana is simply an impossible goal.

The makeup artist is amazing and funny. To keep things simple, Dominika decides she and I should share the prima ballerina dressing room. Everyone else is in the common dressing area, and I would have been too, except Dominika didn't want to have to worry about the timing of the makeup checks.

My face is like nothing I could have done. Thick black arches above my eyes and along my nose ensure that I'm a stark contrast to the light happy fairies. It's beautiful but haunting, like I'm a shadow of someone once beautiful.

The opening is more storytelling than dancing. I watch from the wings as the King and Queen's court go onstage with the baby-doll infant Aurora.

Then the fairies go out in their pastel pancake tutus, carried by male dancers. I watch Andrew with his fairy partner. He is perfectly in sync with the others, smiling, a total professional. My heart surges that he is my friend and doing so well.

Angelique goes on as the Lilac Fairy. She has two solos and the other fairies circle her.

Finally the six corps girls go out for their first dance, including Fiona and Carla. Carla's nerves show on her face, but they all execute the moves perfectly. Still, they do not command your attention. It's easy to see the difference between their presence and that of the fairies, and certainly the Lilac Fairy. Angelique is sublime.

I have quite a wait, as each fairy will give her gift to the baby with a solo, and there will be both male and female corps dances before I finally go on.

I adjust my overdress and make sure the tall horned headpiece is secure and straight.

As the corps dance concludes, the four evil minions who dance with me line up. They are animated and silly, hopping in place. I also do a few *pliés* and *relevés* to make sure I am warm and ready. I have two short pseudo-solos in the prologue. The minions surround me for one, and the fairies for the other, but I am still the focus of the stage.

I try to see out into the audience, but the lighting is too dramatic. I don't want to get too close to the curtain's edge either. The last thing I want is a reprimand for being visible.

I know where Blitz's seats are with his parents. I actually sat in them on the third day of rehearsals here. He's second row, near the middle. The entire front row is filled with business partners and patrons of Alexei.

It doesn't matter that I can't see him. I know he's there.

The dark note arrives in the happy refrain, which is my cue. I step out near the back of the stage, my crow-like minions hurrying around me.

FLASH, a pyrotechnic goes off with the wave of my arms. FLASH FLASH!

Everyone gasps as I come down the steps to the main stage. My head whips back and forth, as if to take in the sight of every person who caused me to be left out of the happy occasion.

The good fairies try to circle around me, as if to apologize for the slight. But I put them off with dramatic movements of my arms. Another FLASH FLASH goes off as my anger surges.

It's different doing it with an audience. I feel their

eyes, their attention. It makes me feel powerful. We had a studio audience on *Dance Blitz*, but they were removed from us, pulled away from the stage and back in the darkness.

There are many more people here. When I pause, I can see the front row, their faces upturned and aglow.

Now comes my longest solo, showing my displeasure and issuing my threat against the baby. I do all the things Franco has taught me for the acting, and not just the arm flourishes and sudden unexpected movements in my dance. But to feel it inside. To bring forward all the anger and vengeance I've ever felt in my life.

Giselle from *Dance Blitz*. Hannah the evil manager. Denham.

My father.

My face contorts as the impressions of all ugly memories surface, fueling my rage and the need to make someone pay.

I curse the child and dance with my minions, gleeful now that I have appeased my need for revenge. We cavort off the stage, caring nothing for the despair we have brought upon the family.

It's what they deserve.

I head all the way offstage and back to the dressing room after the scene. The minions keep their costumes for the entire show, but I have to change into the cloak to look like a peasant in Act 1. The dancers who have come off with me are all bouncy with excitement for getting through our first scene.

I feel pleased myself.

Everything goes perfectly. There are no missed entrances, no falls, no choreography fails. The costumes all work and when we finally go out for our bows, the applause is tremendous.

This is also different. The audience stands and cheers. The curtain rises and falls, then rises and falls again. With more lights up, we can see them out there in suits and evening dresses.

It feels so different. So amazing.

I spot Blitz. He is clapping above his head. Renata is smiling. David scowls as always, but he is nodding, his arms crossed. For some reason this makes me want to laugh.

Aurora and the Prince take a few steps forward one last time, then the curtain closes for good.

Everyone hurries off the stage. Now I'm glad I don't share the main dressing room, as it's mobbed. I couldn't get in there if I tried. I pass the thrown-open doors to head on down to Dominika's. Members of the audience are already starting to come down the hall.

All the principals are expected to attend the meet and greet with the patrons immediately afterward, but we do not wear our costumes. I wonder if I will be able to get rid of the most dramatic of the makeup, the big black sections. I shouldn't have worried. The makeup artist is already there with baby oil and cotton balls to get me ready for the after-party.

I'm not sure what to wear, so I sit while my makeup is changed to see what Dominika puts on. She comes out of the curtained area in a sparkling knee-length gown, and I let out a sigh of relief. I have something similar in the bag I brought.

I overpacked. A full-length gown. A cocktail gown. A pretty dress. And pants and a silk shirt. Then my cutest dance workout clothes.

I come prepared.

"You're all good," the makeup artist says, so I scurry to the dressing area to get out of the black bodice and into normal clothes. Dominika sits to get her makeup refreshed. She sweats a good deal more than I do, but then her parts are much, much harder to perform.

I rush to get in my gown, but then take my time putting on my shoes and sorting my bag while Dominika finishes up. I don't really want to walk to the after-party alone. It's two doors down at a local bar. I'm not sure who will be there.

Suddenly, Dominika is done and heads for the

door. I rush to catch up with her. "It's to the right, isn't it?" I ask her.

She nods. "We can walk together."

I let out a sigh.

But I don't expect the crush of people outside the door. We spend at least ten minutes receiving handshakes and hugs and compliments.

Then I see Blitz.

"You were perfect," he says, lifting me against him. "The most amazing evil fairy ever to grace a stage."

"It was lovely," Renata says, her eyes alight with happiness watching us together. "Just breathtaking."

David grunts his agreement, and Renata elbows him in the side.

"You were good," he says.

"I think we're going to a late dinner," Renata says. "Are you coming?"

"I have to go to a party with the patrons." I glance around and feel chagrin when I realize Dominika has disappeared. I will have to go alone after all.

"I don't want to eat this late," David grumbles. "I'll get indigestion."

"Nonsense," Renata says.

I glance around. The hall is starting to clear. "I think I need to get going."

"Can we drop you off?" Blitz asks.

"It's just two doors down," I say. "I was going to walk with Dominika but I lost her."

"That's our fault," Blitz says. "I can take you."

David sighs heavily, and Renata shoots him a look.

"I'll send my parents off to figure out dinner and I'll walk you down," Blitz says.

"I'm going back to the hotel," David says.

"The limo's out front," Blitz says, ignoring his dad. "I'll send for it later."

With that, we quickly walk away from his parents, ducking our heads like teenagers trying to avoid the chaperones at the dance.

The cool air outside the theater is bliss after the hot crush of the hall.

"Where are we going?" Blitz asks.

"This way," I say. "You didn't get invited? Technically, you should be a patron since you are sponsoring the DVD."

Blitz shrugs. "They might not have liked my negotiations. I left it to Hannah."

"Oh," I say. "That probably didn't make a good impression."

"She gets deals done. I'll let her continue to do my dirty work as long as I don't have to have anything to do with her myself."

We pass a restaurant, and then arrive at a bar. A man stands outside with an iPad, the screen lighting his bushy beard.

"Are you with the ballet?" he asks.

"Yes," I say. "I'm Livia Mays."

He touches my name on the list. "And this is?"

"My date," I say quickly.

A smile quirks on Blitz's lips. It's not often that he isn't recognized. Or maybe this guy has instructions that no celebrity is big enough to get in.

But he nods. "That's fine. Enjoy." He turns and opens the door.

"Sweet," Blitz says. "Crashing a posh ballet party." He takes my arm and slides it through his elbow.

Inside, a long dark-paneled bar stretches along one wall, glittering bottles lining the shelves.

In one corner, a photographer is taking pictures of Dominika and an elegant couple. Great. Hopefully they only want her. I'm not sure I'm up for fake smiling all evening.

Dmitri approaches. "Livia! You are here!" His eyes glance at Blitz and then back to me. "You must meet some of the other patrons."

Blitz and I glance at each other. We both noticed that he didn't greet Blitz. I lean in as we follow Dmitri. "It must have been a really hard bargain," I say.

"I'll check with her tomorrow," he whispers.

Dmitri introduces me to face after face. They begin to blur after a while. They all compliment me on my portrayal of Carabosse. Everyone seems to be neutral about Blitz. No one is upset, nor is anyone excessively interested that I have a TV star as my date.

I take a few pictures, but not as many as Dominika. I'm perfectly happy with that.

After an hour or so, the crowd starts to dwindle.

"Do I get you alone now?" Blitz asks.

"Again?" I ask innocently.

He wraps his arms around me. "Maybe again AND again."

I could be okay with that.

When I see the limo, I burst out laughing.

It is pink.

The door opens, and Carla and Andrew fling themselves out. "It has a hot tub!" she says. Carla is wrapped in a towel and the ends of her hair are wet. "Get in here!"

I peek in. Fiona is taking a turn in the small hot tub, which is inset in a section at the very back of the limo.

"You found one?" I turn to Blitz. "Did your parents ride in this thing?"

"No, it just got here an hour ago. It had to be driven down from Milwaukee. Apparently Chicago is too classy for pink limos with hot tubs."

"I'm never gonna leave!" Carla calls out. She ducks back inside.

I shake my head as I step into the huge interior. I swear the limo goes for the entire city block.

"It's huge," I say as Blitz settles next to me.

"You're not the first girl to notice," he says with a wink.

I shove my shoulder against his.

This is literally the most perfect night.

Chapter Twenty-Four

B litz heads to LA after a couple days. He will catch up with me again when we get to our next city, Boston.

The weeks become a blur. Shows. A few rehearsals for adjustments to the choreography and to practice with the understudies.

Then on a plane to Boston. This time, the girl in charge of travel doesn't bother attempting to put me in first class with the principals, but keeps me back in coach with the rest of the dancers. I'm perfectly fine with that.

A few romances are blooming among the cast members. Fiona gets a super crush on the man who plays Bluebird, which creates some friction with the Princess who dances with him. She's been trying to snag him since auditions. Neither seem to be making big progress. He flirts with both of them, but also seems to have his eye on Andrew.

I've never been around people who are so fluid, liking girls or boys or both. I've just never been around so many people, period.

The stage in Boston is larger, and the extra room really draws out the extra passion and energy from the cast. Blitz comes up with Ted, and we do the limo stuff all over again, this time without a hot tub. Or the pink.

There's a flare-up as we travel to Baltimore, just a bus this time, when Bluebird sits with Andrew. Fiona is devastated and insists she didn't know Andrew OR Bluebird was gay. I don't see how that is possible, as I'm the most sheltered homeschooled girl in the history of sheltered homeschooled girls, and I saw that coming.

So we three girls are hanging tight when we first arrive at rehearsals in the gorgeous facility. I've never been to Maryland. It's August now, and Texas would be brutally hot. But Baltimore is pleasant. I need a sweater in the evenings.

Two days before opening night in the new city, Carla, Fiona, and I go to dinner in an Italian restaurant, risking some carbs since the next day will be mostly wardrobe and understudy rehearsals.

"I don't think I'm ever going to find a man," Fiona

sighs, stabbing at her noodles like they are the enemy.

We're all dressed up, since we've worn nothing but dance clothes for weeks. Carla glitters in a smoky gray sequined tank and black micro-mini. Her brown curls are like a halo around her head.

I'm in a simple ivory sheath but I've put on the tallest stiletto heels imaginable. The restaurant is only two doors down from the hotel, so it is easy enough to do it for one night.

Fiona is fiery in a red satin dress. With her blond hair in a tight chignon, she looks beyond classy.

People glance our way a lot, and I point this out to Fiona. "If you're looking for someone," I tell her, "I think that boy at the bar is working up the courage to send over a drink."

Her head pops up to see who I'm talking about. I've learned to be wary in public, to scan the room for paparazzi or overly zealous fans. Since I've been on the ballet circuit and away from Blitz, the invasions have definitely dropped. Television audiences have short attention spans. I'm grateful.

"He looked at me!" Fiona hisses and ducks her head.

"You don't like him?" Carla asks. She twists in her seat to take a look. "He's cute!"

Fiona stabs another bit of food, but she has eaten

hardly a bite. "I'm too terrified. And I'm only in town for ten days."

Carla and I glance at each other and shrug. There's no helping Fiona. She's miserable wanting them, and terrified when she can have them. I'm guessing she has a story and a past, like all of us. Maybe she'll tell it when she's ready.

"What about you?" I ask Carla. "Do you have your eye on anybody?"

"The Prince is a dream," she says. "But he's married and has two kids."

Fiona leans forward. "I heard he's having an affair with Dominika."

We press our heads together as if the rest of the diners are listening. "How do you know?" Carla whispers.

"I was in the understudy rehearsal when the girl for Aurora was dancing with the Prince. Dominika walked by and looked pretty dang angry when the two of them laughed."

Carla sits back. "That doesn't mean anything." I can tell she doesn't want anyone sullying her dreamy Prince, married or not.

A waiter arrives and sets a glass of wine in front of Fiona. "From the gentleman at the bar," he says.

"Shit!" Fiona says, ducking forward again. "What do I do?"

"Smile at him!" Carla says.

Fiona sits up and gives the boy the cheesiest, fakest grin ever.

"Oh, that will win him over," Carla says.

Fiona smacks her arm.

"Now he knows you're violent," Carla adds.

"I can't take the pressure," Fiona says, standing abruptly. "I'm going to powder my nose."

"Check your snatch," Carla says. "His face might be all up in your business before the night is over!"

Fiona whacks Carla with her evening bag and rushes to the bathroom. I glance over at the boy, who watches her walk, his head tilted in confusion.

"Poor boy," Carla says. "He just wasted ten bucks."

I'm not used to these situations, but they don't make me uncomfortable anymore. Nothing is harder than having dance finalists going on dates with your boyfriend. I rather enjoy being a casual observer, secure that Blitz will be back tomorrow and my own relationship is steady.

"I guess we'll be drunk limo-riding without Andrew," Carla says. "Another friend bites the dust."

"You never know," I say. "Maybe Bluebird will come along."

"His real name is Dusty," Carla says. "But he makes them put Dominic in the program."

We sit in silence for a moment, then Carla says, "I have family near here."

"Really? Are they coming tomorrow?" I ask.

"I don't know. I sent them my two comp tickets but I just don't know." She frowns into her bowl of soup.

"I'm in the same boat in Houston," I tell her. "I have no idea if my best friend will be able to come. She's only seventeen and living at home."

"Are your parents back in Texas?" Carla asks.

"Yes, but I don't expect them. I left home and they took it hard."

Carla sets down her spoon and tugs at an errant curl over her ear. "It's my ex's family up here," she says. "I haven't seen them in two years."

"You want to see him?" I ask.

"I don't know. We're not on good terms." She pushes her bowl away. I can tell this conversation is upsetting her, so I don't pry.

Fiona comes back. The boy sees his opportunity and steps out to greet her.

She pauses to talk.

"Look at that," I say, glad for the distraction.

Fiona turns back to us, but we both wave her to the bar, mouthing, "Go!"

She sits next to him on one of the red velvet stools.

"Success!" Carla says. "Our evening is complete."

We watch Fiona and the boy talk until we're tired of sitting there. We remind her to call us if she needs us, sending the fresh-faced young man, probably twenty or so, a stern look, then head back to the hotel.

In my room, I call Blitz and update him on all the gossip.

"Sounds like you're having fun," he says. "Have you sent your parents the tickets yet?"

"Houston is still six weeks away," I say.

"You should do it soon," he says. "They might have a very busy social calendar."

This makes me laugh. "I love you, Blitz," I say.

"I aim to keep it that way," he says.

"See you tomorrow before the show?" I ask.

"You bet on it," he says.

As I curl up in my bed awaiting my third city's opening night with the ballet, I think of Carla. Her frowns, her preoccupation with men she can't have. And this interesting emotional connection with a mysterious ex.

I'm glad I have her. And that she has me. I have a feeling Baltimore might be a little tough on her.

Like Houston is going to be tough on me.

Chapter Twenty-Five

I manage to peek out into the audience before the show and spot Blitz and Ted in the front row. There are fewer patrons hogging the best seats now that we are deep into the tour.

This crowd is different, more laid back, dressed more casually. I pop back to the dressing room. There are only two community dressing rooms, and I can tell Dominika is annoyed. Ivana has curtained off a small section for her, but the chaos and noise are still very much evident.

The heat seems to build as more dancers shove themselves into the space. I start to wonder if this venue is really meant to house a ballet with a cast our size. Carla squeezes past me for the door, her face pale.

"You okay?" I ask her.

She nods and moves out into the hall.

I'm ready for a break myself so I follow her.

She pauses, glancing at her phone, then heads for the back exit to the alley. I wonder what she's doing, heading outside just ten minutes before curtain.

Carla takes a deep breath, then wrangles with the handle. It pops open finally, a breeze gusting inside. I stop several yards away, partially hidden by a tall wardrobe crate. My concern grows. She really seems upset.

A man comes in, dressed in leather and holding a motorcycle helmet. Then behind him, a little girl about Gabriella's age.

When she sees Carla, she squeals, "Mommy!"

The floor drops out from under me, and I almost lose my balance. Mommy? This is Carla's little girl?

My gaze snaps to the face of my friend. She's so familiar to me after two months of closeness. But she's never mentioned a child. She's seemed too young.

Like I would. I see the lines around her eyes in a new light. She's older than me. And clearly this child of hers doesn't see her often.

"You're a ballerina today!" the little girl says.

"I am," Carla says. "Have you been dancing?"

The child shakes her head. The resemblance between them is clear, the curls, the upturned nose. "Daddy says no dance. I do karate!"

Carla glances up at the man. "Really, Jake? No dance?"

He shrugs. "Dance destroyed us."

Carla bites her lip. She doesn't want to argue with him, I can tell. I've seen that expression in rehearsal.

I want to back away from the scene. But my eyes are on the girl. So lovely. So sweet. How could Carla not want to be near her every single day? What is she thinking? Children grow up. She's missing it.

Now I'm angry and turn away to walk rapidly back down the hall. My dance slippers are silent on the polished floor. Carla might see me now, but I don't care.

I wonder where Gabriella is. I picture her arm outstretched with a ribbon stick. Her smile. Her dark hair crowning her head.

I can't see her anymore. And my best friend just lets her baby's life slip through her fingers.

Everything I left behind rushes back. Dream-catcher Dance Academy. My home. My church. I have nothing to ground me. I'm like a feather dancing on the wind.

I pass the dressing area, the fairies starting to spill out to prepare for the opening number. There's a green room, the door propped open, the laughter of Dmitri and Ivana recognizable from inside.

What have I done? Why am I not fighting? I just

walked away. Maybe Gwen could be reasoned with. I haven't even tried. I am no better than Carla.

I am no better than anyone.

I want air. I need to breathe.

The lights flicker. It's time to go backstage.

But I can't. I have to breathe.

At the other end of the hall is another door to the outside. I pry it open. It leads to an alley that backs a bar. The night is cool, even though the smells assault me. Trash bins. Urine. Broken glass litters the crumbling asphalt.

I step out and immediately feel the bite of something sharp against my foot. I jump back, plucking a shard of a mirror from the side of my slipper.

Frantically, I feel inside the shoe for a cut on my foot. I don't seem to be bleeding.

I'm okay. I'm okay.

The panic washes out the anger, but I'm wrung out, breathing fast. I could have screwed up everything.

I turn back to the door. It's locked from the outside. Great. I can walk through broken glass to the front or just miss my entrance. Maybe I should just walk away. It's what I deserve. I never did make any of the right choices.

I knock on the door, tentatively, not sure anyone can hear me.

But it opens.

It's Andrew. "I thought I saw you come this way!" he says, taking my hand. "What are you doing out there?"

But when I'm in the hall and back in the light, he sees my expression. "Livia, what's wrong? Did something happen?"

I shake my head. I can't say.

Ivana ducks out of the green room and spots us. "Places!" she says to Andrew. "You're about to go on!" She is incensed and glares at me as if his delay is all my fault. Which it is.

He squeezes my hand. "Talk later, okay?" And he turns to rush to the doors to backstage.

"You should get in place too." She glances down. "Your shoe is dirty!"

I turn my shoe. There is a wet stain on the side, shiny against the black.

She grabs my arm and drags me back to the dressing room. "Betty!" she calls out. "We need new slippers for Carabosse!"

Betty pops her head from around a tutu for Red Riding Hood, who has at least an hour before she'll go out. "Right on it." She glances up at the dancer. "Hold tight."

The girl nods.

Betty opens a few drawers in her rolling crate and finds mine. It houses a dozen pairs of black *pointe* shoes, as I go through a pair almost every day. "Here you go, love." She passes the set to me.

Crap. I always break in my shoes in rehearsal so they are not too stiff during the show. But I'll have to make do.

I sit on a stool and rapidly remove the shoes. My tights show a small rip and there is no mistaking the circle of red near my arch on my right foot.

I quickly tuck my leg beneath the layers of my overdress and look around to see if anyone has noticed.

They'll pull me for the understudy if they know. Crap, crap, crap!

"Do you have any black foot tape?" I ask Betty.

She reaches behind her and tosses me a roll.

I listen carefully for the music that is piped in the back to help us hear cues. The fairies are doing their solos. I have two dance numbers until my entrance.

I don't have time to examine the cut or if it is deep. I have to assume it is nothing and go on. I unroll a length of the tape and quickly wind it around my foot to hold together both the tights and the skin around the cut. Thank goodness everything on my costume is black.

"Thank you," I say to Betty. I tuck the soiled slippers under my arm and toss them in a trash can as I leave the room.

I feel the twinge in my instep as I hurry to the

door to backstage. It will be fine. Just a small cut. I'll take care of it after the show.

The minions sigh in relief when I arrive in the holding area to go on. The Lilac Fairy is just concluding her second solo.

"We were getting worried," one of them says.

I just nod and flex my foot. I do a few *relevés* to make sure everything is fine. It is. It's nothing.

The dark note in the music begins and I head onstage for the first flashes of black magic. The minions surround me, and I feel the attention of the crowd on me as I take over the stage.

The dance goes well, the anger, the accusation, the curse.

Then I feel it.

Wetness. Sticky wetness.

I keep going. Finally, the scene ends and I hold my position a moment.

But when I move, I see it. A small smear of blood on the floor.

Oh, no.

I exit the stage as planned with my minions. No one has noticed, and likely won't. It's small, only slightly larger than a quarter.

It's nothing. It has to be.

I hurry through backstage, afraid to step with my right foot, not wanting to leave a trail of blood anyone will notice. My adrenaline is high, so I feel no pain.

When I get out into the light, I do the only thing I can think of to avoid leaving blood on the bright white floor. I go *en pointe*, taking small mincing steps toward the dressing room.

Nobody pays me any mind, rushing back and forth. The suitors hurry past, preparing for their entrance in Act 1. But Dominika spots me.

"Staying warm?" she asks.

I drop down on my left foot, but keep my injured one pointed. "Just a little excited, I guess," I say.

She nods and walks on, unhurried, poised.

Whew.

I peek inside the door of the dressing room. Only a few dancers are here, since Act 1 uses much of the cast.

Betty sits among her boxes, sorting through a box of ribbons.

I can't ask for yet another pair of shoes. I pause near the trash can where I dumped my other slippers. They are surely less bloody than these, even if there is a cut in the side.

When no one is looking, I reach in and grab them.

I walk awkwardly, left foot down and right *en pointe*, until I get to Dominika's curtained area. It is mercifully empty and should be for a while. I still only have a few scenes until I go out to trick her with the spindle. And it's the hardest dance, the one where I must match her.

I have to do this. Have to.

The pain hits me then all at once, as if a switch has been thrown. It's searing and sharp.

I'm done for. I want to cry.

I sink onto a bench, far from the opening of the curtain, and peel off the slipper. Blood has soaked through, seeping through the fabric.

Why did I have to go outside? Why did I let Carla's child upset me?

When I turn my foot to the light, my tights and the tape gleam red on top of the black. I'm not sure what to do about it. I don't think I have time to track down new tights and change.

What have I done?

I take a moment to untape the foot and try to spot the cut. The tights are split now after dancing, and I can see the angry line smeared with red. It's not bleeding now. It's only when I dance.

I try to think. I know I need to clean the wound and bandage it up. I listen to the music again to see where we are. The suitors are done and the corps dancers have come out. There is only their dance and a solo before I go on.

I don't have time to mess with this. I take the tape and wind it tightly on top of the cut now that I know where it is. Thankfully it sticks to itself and isn't wrecked by being bloody. Hopefully that will hold the skin together.

I take the less bloody original shoe. The cut seems so small from the shard of the mirror. I can't believe it did so much damage. I slip it back on, reaching for a box of tissues by the makeup artist's case to wipe up the blood. It's already mostly dry.

"Please don't bleed like crazy," I whisper as I quickly tie on the shoe. I'm perilously close to my entrance. I dash through the dressing room when Betty calls out, "Carabosse! Your peasant cape!"

Shoot. I have a costume change.

But Betty is good. She rapidly removes the black overdress and ties on the peasant disguise. I rush out, my adrenaline surging and blasting away the pain, and hurry backstage.

The music cue is already going, but it's not too bad. I push through and go straight out onstage, then slow down for my menacing walk that gives me away to the audience.

Did I think the pain was gone? As I walk forward toward the bright front of the stage where Aurora waits to be tricked by my spindle, the pain is a jagged force, blasting up my leg with every step.

But the show must go on. I didn't call in my understudy. I decided to do this myself. I must block out everything but the dance.

I circle her, offering the spindle, but she turns away.

Then we dance, push, pull, forward, back, until it's time to match our steps, my triumphant deceit.

But when I hold the long, slow turn *en pointe* on the injured foot, it just gives way. The position doesn't hold. I drop my *pointe* before Dominika, and fail to get back up in it.

We take three steps and are supposed to match another *en pointe*, but my foot simply won't go. I stay flat-footed to her *pointe* but keep my composure. The audience won't know. They'll assume Carabosse is no dance match for the beautiful Aurora.

But Ivana will.

And Dominika.

I feel sick. My mind races ahead to all the moves. Another right *en pointe*. I try to force my body up, and it goes, thank God, but holding it makes me feel absolutely faint.

The scene will never end.

I muck through it, knowing I'm not sharp or beautiful but clunky and misfiring.

Finally Dominika, her eyes blazing at me, takes the spindle and pricks her finger. As she falls, I back away, dropping the peasant cape away to reveal my identity.

The court rushes forward as I make my exit. I'm

nowhere near as expressive and gleeful as usual as I head offstage. I can barely hold myself together.

I'm instantly caught by Evangeline. "What happened out there?" she asks. To her credit, she sounds more concerned than angry.

Unlike Ivana. As Evangeline and a male dancer help me out into the hall, she storms up to me.

"What was that horrifying performance? What is wrong with you?" She lifts her arm almost as if she's going to strike me.

The male dancer steps between us. "She's bleeding," he says.

Ivana glances down. Then she smiles. "I'll call your understudy," she says.

She's thrilled.

Chapter Twenty-Six

T he second act goes on without me. There isn't much for the understudy to do in that part. Just be pushed out of the bedroom by the Lilac Fairy. Still, it hurts to be replaced. I text Blitz, who immediately abandons his seat and comes backstage.

The nurse who travels with us cleans the wound and wraps it. "I wouldn't dance on this for a couple days," she says. "But it's a small cut. It only bled so much because you were dancing. It's nothing that knocks you out for the season. I've seen blisters that were worse." She pats my leg.

"I don't care," Ivana says. "She's out. She was barely keeping up before, there's no way she'll do it now."

I don't know who she's talking to. She's the highest-ranking person back here. Dmitri and Alexei are still watching the ballet in the seats. Maybe she's getting her argument ready.

But Blitz is here, and he's pissed at her attitude. "If she's not in the New York production for the DVD recording, I'm backing out of the deal," he says smoothly. "The contract explicitly states that Livia must be Carabosse."

"I couldn't care less about your DVD," Ivana snaps back. "Classical dance isn't improved by camera angles and close-ups."

I can't look at anybody. They're arguing my fate like I'm the sleeping princess, not the powerful villain. Yet, I say nothing. I don't want to admit that I went outside after getting upset and let this happen. I have handed Ivana the opportunity she was looking for.

"Protocol will be to call a meeting of the financial backers before you kill a major deal like that," Blitz says. "You're cutting out a lot of money for a lot of people, including yourself."

"I don't do choreography for the money," she says. "I do it for love. You television people will never understand that."

I want to walk away from this scene, but my foot is wrapped and propped on a chair. The nurse has busied herself with putting things away.

Blitz looms over us, his arms crossed.

Ivana leaps from her chair. "I have more important things to do than babysit a silly girl," she says. "We are almost to the end of the ballet."

I can breathe easier once she's gone. The nurse pats my leg and heads for her little corner of the dressing room.

The dancers who serve as my minions come in. They have nothing else to do until the curtain call. I guess my understudy will do that for me.

"You okay, Livia?" one of them asks, a friendly man who leads them. He lifts his crow mask.

"Just a little cut. I'm out for a couple days."

The rest of them nod, their black beaks bobbing up and down. "Glad to hear it's not serious," another one says. I'm not sure which one in all those feathers.

They head back to the stage area to await the curtain call. The big wedding dance is happening. It's very close to over.

Blitz kneels next to me. "You want me to take you back to the hotel?"

"Okay," I say. "What about Ted?"

"We have a local driver. We can wait in the limo."

I heave myself up, keeping my injured foot off the floor. Blitz stands. I lean on him to head to the costume rack to leave my tutu and bodice for tomorrow. After a few awkward steps, though, Blitz scoops me up in his arms, costume and all.

The tutu slides up and almost hits him on the nose. "Dangerous business, carrying dancers," he says.

"It's easier on your shoulder. That's why they do it that way in the show."

He shifts me on his arm, then his hand on my butt lifts me to his shoulder.

"Huh," he says. "It is easier." The tutu goes off to one side now.

We head to the curtains. If I hurry, I can be changed and gone before the others arrive. I still don't know if Carla saw me witness the moment with her daughter.

Even thinking the word makes my stomach drop. I don't know how to look at her. I'm sure she has a story. We all have stories. But it's so hard.

But now I get why she was so subdued at dinner last night. She must have known she'd see the little girl, who obviously lives with her father.

Who doesn't allow her to dance. What did he say? Dance was what destroyed them?

Blitz sets me down carefully and I quickly strip off the bodice and tutu. The tights are ruined, so I peel them off and tug them over the bandage. The nurse had already cut the foot of them away.

Blitz watches every movement. "Do you always get this naked in community dressing rooms?" I only wear a thong now.

"Only if everyone is watching me," I say, turning to dig in my bag for a pair of silky workout pants and a T-shirt.

Blitz lets out a groan. "You're killing me."

"I'm just kidding," I tell him. "But you do learn not to be too shy. There's other curtained areas, and bathrooms with stalls. You can find places to go."

I don't tell him how we all have to try on our costumes in a big fitting area and you never know when a seamstress is just going to remove your top unexpectedly to change something.

The noise level increases. The show has ended. I jerk my T-shirt over my head and sit down to pull on the pants. By the time dancers start filling the room beyond the curtain, I have zipped up the bag.

"Shall I carry you again?" Blitz asks.

"I don't want to be obvious," I say. "But I will let you take these out to the costume manager. Large woman with a beehive."

He nods and takes the tutu and bodice.

I stand up and test my foot. It doesn't really hurt, but the bandage makes it impossible to fit my shoe on. I rummage through my bag and pull out a pair of plain ballet slippers, the sort you warm up in. I think they might fit.

They do, and I instantly feel better.

Blitz ducks back inside just as the makeup artist also appears.

"Do you need me to get you ready for the after-party?" she asks.

"No," I say. "I'm not going."

DEANNA ROY

"Why did you not do the final scene? Her makeup was completely different from yours since I didn't do it."

I point to my foot. "I got a small injury. I'll be out a few days."

"Oh!" she glances down. "So you won't need me tomorrow?"

"I don't think so. I'll let you know how it all goes down."

She nods.

I put my arm around Blitz's. "I guess carrying me is the easiest thing," I say to him.

"I'll make it look like I'm rescuing you from your drudgery, like in that movie *An Officer and a Gentleman*."

"I haven't seen it," I say.

"I only saw the *Simpsons* version of the scene," he says with a laugh. "But I get the gist."

Only a few of the dancers turn to look as Blitz sweeps me up and carries me across the dressing room. We head out the back hall door, not the bar side, but the one where Carla was. There's a small parking lot for theater staff only.

Ted is already there with the limo. He's not driving, but sitting in the back. He scoots over as Blitz deposits me on the end of the seat. I push around to make room for Blitz.

"Some other girl was you at the end!" Ted says. "What happened?"

"Injured," I say. My face flushes as I realize how many people will ask. And I can't tell them the whole story.

"How long will you be out?" Ted's face is full of concern.

"Just a few days."

"Well, that's good."

The driver closes the door. Soon we're pulling away from the building and crossing through the throng pouring out the exits.

I lay my head against Blitz's. Only now that we're away from everyone do I start to feel everything. The sting of the cut. The tightness of the wrap. The downward pull of the thoughts of Gabriella. The grief that I will not be performing tomorrow.

I should have known I would screw this up too.

Chapter Twenty-Seven

Despite how much it bled, the cut really isn't much. Blitz and I lounge around his hotel room, me walking every now and then to test it. I don't really feel anything.

But I'm not sure of my status with the troupe. No one has called to tell me what will happen. I'm not even sure who makes that decision. Surely not Ivana. If it is, then I'm out.

"Man, ballet really is a different world from TV," Blitz says. He's perched on the sofa, intent on his phone.

"How so?" I ask, feeling my anxiety soften just looking at him in a pale blue T-shirt and jeans, no shoes. I think I will ask him to finish the tour with me, if he can. If I'm still on it. I want him close.

"Well, when a girl in season one fell on my show,

there were six zillion Tweets about it, news shows picked it up, and the studio got flooded with flowers and messages," he says.

"You think I should be on every network news?" I ask. He's funny about things like this, as if it really matters.

"No, I just find it interesting."

"Why are you searching so hard?" I scoot closer to him and lay my head on his shoulder. It's after noon, but I haven't bothered to get dressed, wrapped up in a hotel robe after a bath where I kept my foot out of the water.

"Just looking for bargaining chips," he says. "I'm not going to let that chick kick you off the show. The DVD is worthless without you. Have you seen the sales on these other ballets? Peanuts."

"I think ballet is probably best live onstage," I say.

"Nonsense," he says. "It's elitist. Not everyone can afford a ticket. And tons of people live in places where there isn't a ballet for two hundred miles."

"So what are you going to do about it?" I ask.

"Start a shit storm," he says. "Make sure they remember you're important." He taps angrily at the phone.

I cover the screen with my hand and push the phone to his lap. "Don't Tweet me," I say. "It's fine. We'll talk to Dmitri and figure this out."

He wraps his arm around my shoulders and draws me in even closer. "I guess you do have to live with these people."

Even Carla, I think. So weird how many times we'd talked in our rooms or on airplanes or waiting for our scenes in the rehearsal space, and she never mentioned she was a mother.

Of course, I didn't either.

I wonder if she looked me up after we met and saw the gossip about my secret baby. It had mostly died down by the time we left for rehearsals, but it's definitely something that pops up when you Google Livia Mays.

Blitz and I didn't really talk about what happened last night. I was tired and strung out. He always respects my need to think during this time and doesn't push.

But now he finally asks, "So where was the glass that cut you?"

I close my eyes. "Outside in the alley."

"You went outside?"

"I needed some air." I shift against him, my fingers plucking anxiously at the soft belt of the robe. "It gets really crowded backstage."

"This was before the show?" he asks.

"Yes. I realized I was hurt but tried to dance through it. It just bled more than I thought."

"You going to try and practice tomorrow?"

"I'll do some stretches and light work. Probably not *pointe*. I'll see the regular trainer and let him tell me what to do. Unless I'm really fired."

He just accepts my explanation. I could tell him about Carla, but it's really not my secret to reveal. And the why doesn't matter.

My phone rings from the bedroom.

Blitz jumps up. "I'll get it. You stay still."

When he comes back, he says, "Looks like Dmitri."

I lay my head back. "Can I ignore all this?"

Blitz smiles and taps my screen. "This is Livia's management agent," he says.

Then laughs, "Yeah, it's just me."

Then "Let me ask her."

He presses mute. "You want to talk to him? He's checking on how you are."

I shake my head no.

Blitz returns to the call. "She's resting from her injury." When I sit up, he quickly adds, "Her very minor, not very bothersome injury. Really, she was up all night reviewing her moves on this very important role she has."

God, Blitz! I reach for the phone.

"Actually, here she is." He makes a "sorry" face while he passes the phone.

"Hello?" I say.

"Livia!" Dmitri says. "How is our Carabosse?"

"I'm fine," I say. "The nurse says I can dance in a couple of days."

"Good to hear," he says. "I guess you know Ivana is very concerned about your ability to dance."

I slide back onto the cushions to stare at the ceiling. "I got that feeling last night."

"We want you back on the tour before New York, so we're hoping everything looks good by next weekend to close out the shows here."

"Blitz is concerned about having a different Carabosse on the recordings for the DVD," I tell him.

"We all are," he says. "But Dominika does have a clause about her principal dancers. We're hoping you will impress her upon your return so that everyone's concerns are laid to rest."

"I intend to," I say.

"Very good. You rest today. We'll see you soon."

I shut off the call and drop the phone on the carpet. "Great," I say.

"What's going on?" Blitz sits on the floor by the sofa.

"I have to be approved to come back on the show. By Dominika."

"I knew we should have eliminated that clause. You think Ivana will try to pressure her to kick you off?"

I shrug and cover my eyes with my arm. "Probably."

"I thought you and Dominika were getting to be chums," he says. "Sharing a makeup girl and all."

"I don't know," I say. "I don't know anything."

He strokes my hair. "It will be fine, Livia. One way or another, we'll get past this."

My eyes smart. This has been the worst summer. Just the worst. All the grief and frustration swirls together. I can't seem to separate them anymore. My family. Gabriella. The harshness of dancing with a troupe.

I roll into the back of the sofa to block out everything, even the beautiful room, even Blitz.

But Blitz knows me. He gets it. His body takes up the space I've left on the cushions to curl up behind me. I'm cocooned, safe, protected.

I can't let this overwhelm me. I just have to keep going.

Chapter Twenty-Eight

✿❀✿

Despite the nurse's encouragement to stay off my feet for two to three days, I go into rehearsals on Monday in my dance clothes.

Blitz comes with me, along with Ted. My "manager" and my "bodyguard" create a little entourage to back me up throughout the day.

The trainer checks me out first, announces, "It's just a flesh wound!" and says to dance without *pointe* or *demi-pointe* for an hour and come back.

So we head to a small warm-up room, avoiding the stage where my understudy is rehearsing with the cast, and I run through some of the scenes by myself or with Blitz when I can, keeping it easy.

Carla, Fiona, and Andrew are naturally tied up with the main group, but as soon as they break, all three of them rush into my room.

"What happened?" Fiona asks, dropping to her knees to examine my dance slipper.

"A piece of glass cut me," I say. "It's nothing."

Andrew gives me a big hug. I notice Carla hanging back by the door, as if she only came because she couldn't come up with a reason to tell the others why she shouldn't. Her hesitation tells me she did spot me walking down the hall while she hugged her daughter. When she sees me looking, she gives a little wave.

"I'm about to go back to the trainer," I say. "He wants to check it periodically as I start slowly dancing again."

Fiona touches the bandage wrapped around my instep, its whiteness stark next to the pink of my slipper. "I do hope you get to come back," she says.

I don't want to badmouth Ivana or mention the ultimatum.

"I will," I say.

"We have to get to props," Carla says. "We're getting new spring wreaths for New York. For the DVD." She glances over at Blitz. "Something splashier."

"Have fun with that," I say.

Fiona hops up and leans in for another hug. "I'll text you tonight!" she says.

"Looks like some good friends," Ted says when they leave. "The blond one is cute."

"Down, boy," Blitz says. "Don't be macking on Livia's dance friends."

I slide into an easy stretch, hiding my smile. I could see Fiona with Ted. Her wine-buyer at the restaurant the other night hadn't worked out. He tried to kiss her and she said it was like getting licked by a dog, and not in a good way. She escaped.

"We missed our limo party," I say. "Ted could have come along."

"I'm always down for a limo party," he says.

"We'll do it next weekend after your triumphant return," Blitz says. He walks over and presses on my back to deepen my stretch. "Foot feeling okay?"

"Just fine." I lift it and rotate my ankle. "Maybe a little twinge."

"Let's go see the trainer again," Blitz says. "It's been an hour."

We head down the hall and the trainer says the foot is holding up well, but still no *pointe* for today. We drift off to head to lunch. It feels strange to have no schedule, no dances, no direct pressure to do anything.

I'm torn between going back to prove that I'm determined to return to the stage and blowing off the rest of the day to spend it with Blitz and Ted. When we leave the cafe, I'm still not sure what to do.

"Should I dance more?" I ask Blitz.

He knows what's going through my mind. "If

you're injured more, you're out, but if you give Ivana more fuel by skipping, you could be out." His face is thoughtful. "So really the only option is to dance and not get hurt."

Ted sniffs. "If it were me, I'd storm into the rehearsals and give my replacement the stink eye. Make everybody remember I'm here, and I'm pissed."

Blitz laughs and slaps Ted on the back. "I knew there was a reason I kept you around. Should we go with her, O wise adviser?"

"Damn straight," Ted says. "We'll stand on either side of the stage like evil gargoyles ready to curse the whole lot of them."

"Awesome," Blitz says. "I'm in."

So we head back to the theater. We've gone ahead of the cast, so when we arrive, the only people there are Dominika, the Prince, and the pianist.

Dominika looks surprised to see me, but she's polite as always. "How is your foot?" she asks.

"Doing great," I say. "The trainer had me dance this morning and it stayed nice and closed. Should be fine by tomorrow."

I don't know that this is true, but I like the uncomfortable look it gives her.

The Prince gives a bit of a sneer. "Ophelia is doing great in your place," he says.

"She's a great dancer," I say. "I'm glad she got to perform the role yesterday. She deserved it."

We're in a standoff. I can tell by Blitz's expression that he's pleased with how I'm handling it.

Despite what the trainer said, I can't help but take it a step further. "Dominika, can we run through that one part of the spindle scene? I feel like I still have a little ways to go to match my form to yours."

Now Blitz isn't as pleased looking. I'm not supposed to do *pointe* today. But I slide my bag around me and pull out my toe shoes. Sometimes things are worth the risk. If I want to keep this role, I have to prove myself.

"Is she pulling a Black Swan?" Ted asks.

Blitz laughs. "It's only a flesh wound," he says.

My gaze shoots daggers at him even though Dominika's quizzical look tells me she doesn't understand what he's saying. It doesn't translate for her.

Ted steps back to stand beside the base of the stage, his arms crossed and his expression stern. Gargoyle pose. Blitz follows his lead and stands on the other side.

I'm not admitting this to them, but I know that by the time I put on shoes and warm up, I'll be dancing ten minutes tops before people start coming in. It's a calculated risk, one designed to impress.

I slide the *pointe* shoes on as if it's no big deal that I bled on this stage just two nights ago. Inside, I'm anxious. What if the cut breaks open? If I bleed again, that will be it.

I have to trust the trainer, the nurse, my instincts. It will be okay.

Dominika and the Prince continue their practice while I do a quick warm-up. It won't help me prove myself with my injury if I strain a tendon in the process.

I take a deep breath and do my first *relevé*, hoping my foot holds up. It feels fine, so I come out and do a few more. Okay, it's working.

I decide to minimize any more *relevés* to avoid too much *pointe* work before doing the hard movements with Dominika.

When the dance with the Prince ends, they look over at me. I nod to the pianist. He shifts his papers around and starts the opening notes to the spindle scene.

We've done this so many times that I know each note, each phrase, by heart, no matter if it's a piano or a recording or a full orchestra.

I scurry away from her so I can make the entrance at the back of the stage, approaching with caution and stealth, but enough creepy evil that the audience recognizes me. I'm well practiced at this, and the acting coach Franco says I do the part well.

Then the initial approach. I realize I don't have a prop for the spindle and mime it. Dominika shies away, and I hear Ted say, "This is great stuff."

On the second approach we begin our push and pull. Then I try to convince her to take the spindle.

This time when I go up *en pointe*, I feel the twinge again. But nothing is wet, no searing pain. I keep going.

It's a challenging scene. A few dancers enter, and I settle down a little. I will only have to get through this one time and I'll prove myself.

By the time we get to the hardest part of all, where I must match Dominika's style, the front rows are filled with dancers. I don't have time to look at their faces or see if Ivana has entered. I concentrate fiercely on my movements, determined to make this rehearsal the best I've ever done, despite the fear, the risk, and some pain.

It's still not perfect, but it's another step up from where I've been. When we get to the end of the scene and Dominika collapses, the pianist stops.

The dancers all clap, which sometimes happens during rehearsal, but not often. I finally look around. The corps dancers are there, happy that I'm back, including a shining-faced Fiona and relieved Andrew.

Then Ophelia, the understudy, arms crossed and scowling. Then Ivana, looking annoyed.

We've reviewed the contract. Ivana can't fire me. Just Dominika has that power. Otherwise only a doctor saying I'm out for injury, or noncompliance with rehearsal or misconduct, can oust my position.

Dominika glances at Ivana. "I hate dance politics," she says. "If she's well enough to dance, she dances."

"I want her cleared through the trainer first," Ivana says. "I won't have permanent damage to her foot on my head."

I'm perfectly relieved to hear this. I don't really want to dance for several hours more, not yet.

"I'm glad to check in with him again," I say. "I'll do as he says."

Blitz and Ted still stand below, but they aren't all serious anymore. Blitz is positively giddy.

I pick up my dance bag and wave to everyone. I pause by Ophelia. "Thank you so much for standing in for me yesterday," I tell her. "You do beautiful work."

She can't very well scowl at me for that in front of the entire company, so she nods and relaxes her expression.

I quickly walk to the door, casually tossing my bag on my shoulder, super careful to show zero evidence of pain or injury as I head out.

I've pulled it off.

Chapter Twenty-Nine

❧❀❧

Another day of rest is really all I needed, and I'm back to full rehearsals by Wednesday. The cast settles back in with me as Carabosse, and even as we do our last performances in Baltimore, we prepare for the adjustments to the stage and props for the longest run of the ballet in New York.

My twentieth birthday marks our second night in the Big Apple. As a gift to me and the whole cast, Blitz buys tickets for everyone to the New York City Ballet's production of *Swan Lake*, which has just opened for the start of their fall season.

It's a big night as everyone dresses up to see the dream career for a ballerina. Dancers begin training at age six with the School of American Ballet housed across the street from Lincoln Theater.

None of us will ever dance on this stage, as their

apprentices are taken very strictly from their own school.

So watching *Swan Lake* is bittersweet for many of the cast, since it is too late for any of us to be a part of this ballet tradition. I sit with Blitz and Ted, who will be helping as a driver and security as we start the DVD shooting in a few days. Our seats are low and center, as I wanted to be right up on the dancers. Most of the cast is scattered throughout, whatever last-minute seats Blitz's assistant Shelly could gather up at such a late date.

I look around during intermission, spotting friends and cast members chatting in clumps. Many of them approach me for hugs and to wish me a happy birthday. I feel very much like the belle of the ball, a complete turnaround from Baltimore.

Andrew stays close to Bluebird. Fiona and Carla hang out with them. Carla sees me looking and glances away. I'm not sure how to bridge the gap between us. We should talk about it, but now that I'm staying with Blitz full-time, there never seems to be an opportunity.

We settle in for the last part of the ballet, where Odette realizes she has been betrayed and will be a swan forever. I hold on to Blitz's hand. It's interesting to me how so many of these classic ballets revolve around love. At least *Sleeping Beauty* isn't tragic.

After it's over, Blitz and I escape in the limo to Times Square.

I've never been to New York and feel overwhelmed by the crowds and blazing signs. There are so many people everywhere. Each sidewalk requires careful navigation or you get pushed into the street or jostled by people walking faster than you.

Blitz takes us to a set of red stairs that lead to nowhere. They are lit and covered with literally hundreds of tired tourists just taking in the sights.

"I love it here," Blitz says, leading me to the top. "It's one of the few places in the world that matches my level of high-octane energy."

I believe it. From atop the steps, we can see everything, the blinking signs, the giant screens flashing commercials and news. Lines of taxis fill the streets as people pour out of theaters and try to find their way home.

"Well, look at that," Blitz says. "I think New York is happy to have you."

He turns me and points to a TV screen so huge it takes up half the height of a skyscraper. An image of him and me flashes onscreen. We kiss, and fireworks light up the image and it reads "Happy 20th Birthday, Livia."

I squeal. "How did you do that?"

He bows. "Anything for my love!"

"This is the most amazing thing!" I exclaim. I can't even take it all in.

But, as almost always happens in crowds, we're spotted, and suddenly cell phones are lighting up.

"Blitz Craven! Over here!"

"Livia is with him!"

"Will you sign this?"

The rush begins, and we could easily get trapped on the steps.

But Blitz thinks quickly and lifts me up on his shoulder. The wide pleated skirt of my blue dress covers his arm and chest in his suit jacket.

I know what he's thinking and immediately roll across his chest, landing lightly on a stair and spinning out.

People back away to give us space to dance, cell phones in the air.

We make our way down the steps, the crowd parting to let us dance by. A couple guys with bongos start a beat and we match it. The moves are simple, things we could do in our sleep. Lift, turn, step step step, out, in, and then do it all over again.

But it's enough for the crowd. When we get to the bottom, we bow and quickly dive into the walking masses. Everyone's too busy figuring out if they got good footage for many to follow, and soon we're back in the flow and anonymous again.

"Should have brought a hat," Blitz says.

"That wasn't too bad. You were brilliant."

Blitz squeezes my hand. "I try."

"Did you talk to the director of the DVD today?" I ask.

"Yep, while you were in rehearsal. We're all square for filming on Tuesday."

It'll be fun to be somewhat back in our world. I won't feel quite so subservient to Ivana.

"Have you given thought to Houston yet?" Blitz asks.

I frown. We're away from all the bright lights, just walking along souvenir shops and late-night diners. "You mean the tickets for my parents?"

"Yes, those."

"I'll mail them tomorrow," I say.

"You've been saying that for weeks." He slides his hand through the crook of my arm.

"I know."

"What are you more afraid of? That they won't come? Or that they will?"

I picture my dad calling me a dirty whore in front of Ivana and snort. "I don't know. Both are bad."

"Do it for Andy. He'd love to see his big sister dance."

I know Blitz is right.

He squeezes my hand. "How about we go back to the hotel and have crazy porn sex, then we'll put those tickets in an envelope? It's your birthday. It's a lucky day. What do you say?"

Blitz makes me laugh. "Okay."

"That's my princess," he says. He's about to correct himself when I cut him off.

"It's okay to call me Princess," I tell him. "I was just upset then."

"Good," he says. "Because I was going to start calling you Porn Star instead."

I smack him on the arm, which he totally deserves, but he makes me laugh. Having Blitz helps me think less about my first birthday without the people who gave birth to me.

Chapter Thirty

The filming is fun. The addition of cameras and crew at our dress rehearsals, plus the thrill of being in New York, add to the overall excitement of the cast.

Andrew, Fiona, and I get in the habit of hanging out with Blitz and the director to look at the new footage, which they call the "roughs." We all start picking up lingo, more than I learned from *Dance Blitz*. I never really got to hang out with the film crew back then since the director was so daunting.

They work to solve the sound problems of the hard toe of new *pointe* shoes banging on the floor. There is also echo effect from the orchestra, since there's no audience members present to absorb the sound. They finally agree to record the music separately during a live show. It saves them having to add in applause. Apparently the old footage and new sound will be matched up in "post."

New York is probably the most fun segment of the tour. I feel like a part of the process, an important piece, rather than just the worst-trained member of the troupe who got a part based on fame.

Blitz decides to travel back to LA for a few days with the production team, skipping Miami. We will meet back up again in Houston. I have no way of knowing what happened to the tickets I sent Mom and Dad. After they were mailed, I panicked that Mom would talk to Mindy's mother and the jig would be up on the ballet prize for the other family, keeping my friend from coming.

But Mindy keeps in touch via text on the phone we slipped her before the tour. Her parents don't have any idea yet that I am in the show, only that they have ballet tickets and a hotel room. The two families still aren't on solid speaking terms, even though they do greet each other at church every Sunday.

Mindy reports that my parents seem sadder lately, less involved than before. She hopes they will come to the ballet. The relationship really needs to be repaired for anyone to be happy.

I thought for a while to try sending Gwen tickets as well, but never told Blitz my idea. Probably once she realized I was in the cast, she would either not come or be resentful of my continued interference. I don't know if I can do anything to see my daughter again. Fourteen years is so long.

On the flight from Miami to Texas, Carla ends up on my row. We haven't specifically avoided each other since that moment in Baltimore when I ran from her and her daughter and injured my foot in the alley. But we haven't said more than simple greetings or compliments on a performance since then.

But it's hard for me to stay silent. I hurt so much for my loss. I have to know what keeps her away, why she would choose that, or if she is forced to, like I am. If so, it's something we have in common.

We sit in coach with three seats to a side, and one of the fairies is between us. But the other girl quickly puts on headphones and zones out, leaving me and Carla to flip through magazines and avoid eye contact.

After takeoff, and once the beverage cart has passed, I finally work up enough courage to say, "Your little girl is lovely."

Carla stiffens, staring down at the pages in her hands.

I think she isn't going to respond, and that will be it, when she finally says, "Her father is better for her than I am."

This makes my belly tighten. "Did he take her from you?"

She can't meet my gaze and looks out the window instead. "I was a dancer. It's all I ever wanted to do. When she arrived, I got so out of shape. I had to work hard to get back in it."

"You were young, though."

With this, she turns back. "I'm not as young as you think. I was twenty-three when she was born."

"So you left her with her dad?"

Her chin drops and she stares at the magazine again. "He is really good with her. I was gone, chasing any dance audition I could get. I wasn't home."

"So you two split up?"

"We were never married. There's no custody agreement. No legal tangle. I just chose dance. It's what I wanted."

I have to look away. I can't believe it's so simple. She had a daughter and she left her.

We don't speak again. We might never speak again. I know she made choices the best she knew how. Maybe she would judge me for the adoption. But I have a hard time thinking about the little girl she can have back at any moment, if she would just put her first.

The plane touches down at the airport and the pilot announces that it is 102 degrees. Everyone groans. That's Texas for you. Even though summer is officially over, the weather often doesn't break until October.

I realize that while I was away, Gabriella started kindergarten. It hits me what I'm missing, what I've already missed. At least before all this happened, Blitz and dancing and fame, I could see pictures on Facebook. Then for nine miraculous months, I taught her dance class.

Now, I have nothing.

I want to lash out at Carla. Tell her how selfish she is. How stupid.

But who am I to judge anyone?

The aisle fills with dancers tugging down their carry-ons. The girl between me and Carla takes off her headphones and looks around.

When I get out, I load up on the bus to the hotel and sit in the front with Betty from wardrobe and other members of the crew. I'm not up for speaking to anyone.

The heat and the smells all make me think of home. I grew up here, before I got pregnant. This is where I knew Denham. Where I had a normal life. If I could go back, I would change things.

But not getting pregnant. Not Gabriella. I could never change the circumstances that brought her here.

I wouldn't give her up.

Although, then I wouldn't meet Blitz.

It's so hard to know what path was the right one. And it's pointless. I can't actually change anything.

And I can't willingly give up the parts of my life I love now.

When we get to the hotel, I call a ride share so I can head out into the city alone. Blitz will arrive in the morning, but tonight is all mine to revisit the places I once knew.

I give the young woman driving a yellow Beetle with daisies on the hood the address to my old house.

"You sure?" she asks as she puts it in her phone and tilts her head at the location that pops up. "That's a really bad part of town."

"I grew up in that house," I tell her. "I moved six years ago."

She shrugs. "It probably hasn't changed that much, then."

I think about this as we navigate rush-hour traffic. Was it bad then? I was old enough to know when we left, a freshman in high school. Sure, there were car break-ins and burglaries, and the known drug dealers on a couple corners. This all seemed normal and manageable at the time.

But as we exit the highway and approach the seedy neighborhood, I see it all with completely different eyes. Everything is the same, from the pawn shop with its iron-barred windows to the weedy empty corner lot where I would fly kites. The convenience store has a new name but is otherwise exactly as I remember it.

But I've changed. I see the poverty here. The brokenness. The people who work too many hours, have too many problems. They can't worry about keeping up lawns or getting rid of junked-out cars. Their dogs bark behind chain-link fences, and their kids roam the cracked sidewalks.

Everyone here is barely surviving.

I feel like an outsider.

I am one.

I'm glad this car is low-key, the sort of thing some dad would buy cheap and paint himself for his daughter. It fits in. We don't evoke any stares, well, at least nothing more than amusement at the daisies, as we head down my old street.

My heart is actually pounding as we approach the old house. It looks terrible to me now. Small and falling apart, one of the porch columns so rotted through, it's splintered at the base.

Whoever lives there now has a bunch of kids, or one terribly messy one, as the scraggly dead grass is littered with balls and cracked plastic toys, faded from the sun.

But I can see myself on the porch. I picture friends walking up, the path to school, light in the windows.

The girl has stopped in front of it. "You just want to look?" she asks.

"For a minute," I say.

The fence is in worse shape than in my day, the metal poles listing to one side. It makes me sad, seeing it, and I get this wild idea of buying it and fixing it up again.

Then the feeling passes. Terrible things happened there. I'm glad I can't see the backyard, where I came in that awful night when I thought Denham was my brother.

I shake my head. This is enough. "We can go," I say.

The car eases down the narrow street, half blocked with cars parked along the curbs. I realize we're going to pass the house that had the travel trailer in back. Gabriella was probably conceived there. And my stomach falls again.

I decide not to look, not to think anymore. I rest my head on the back of the seat and remember New York, Times Square, the ballet, Lincoln Theater.

"You want to go back to your hotel now?" the girl asks.

"Yes," I say.

There's nothing for me here anymore. If there ever was. Just dusty memories and decaying history.

Moving forward is the only way to go. The only question is, will my family come and be a part of my future?

Chapter Thirty-One

M y nerves for this opening night are much worse than the first. I keep walking to the exit doors closest to the stage, peering in at the seats to see if my parents have come.

I get two warnings from security that the dancers are not allowed to be seen by the crowd. This is Dmitri's rule, I know, a superstition about bad luck.

The second time, I head on back, relying on texts from Blitz. He's incognito in a Derby hat, trying not to be spotted by my family if they do come.

I text him every thirty seconds, and he's good about responding back until about fifteen minutes before the curtain call. I wonder if something has happened, and write him again and again.

Then someone taps me on the shoulder. "You're wanted in the hall," Bluebird says. I try to think of him as Dominic now that I know his name, but still, my mind goes to Bluebird first.

I follow him out of the principals dressing room.

And I see Mindy!

"You're here!" I say. "Did your parents figure it out?"

"They apparently knew weeks ago," she says. "But we came anyway." She looks so grown up in a sparkly black dress. Her light brown hair looks sun-kissed, and she's tan.

"How is Cowboy?"

"Good!" she says. "I still haven't told my parents about him. But we get to do rides together at the barn."

"How did you get back here?" I ask.

"Blitz brought me!"

We both turn to look for him, but he's down the hall and just gives a little wave.

Now that the thrill of seeing her has calmed a bit, I have to ask, "Did my parents use their tickets? They are close to you."

Mindy frowns. "They weren't there when I left. We don't really talk at church, so I don't know anything."

I nod. "It's okay. I'm so glad you could make it."

The lights dim, then brighten.

"Oh," I say, "you need to get back!"

"I can't wait to see you up there!" she says, hurrying back to Blitz. "I'll see you after?"

"Yes, let Blitz find you again!" I wave as he takes her down the hall and back through to the seating.

It's so good to see her, as if I've reconnected a missing piece of myself.

"Places!" Ivana calls. "Curtain in five!"

I head back to the dressing room to wait until closer to my entrance to go backstage. I need to warm up a little more. I want to be perfect tonight. If not for my parents, at least for Mindy and her family. The only guests of my own I've had this whole tour were Blitz's family and Ted.

The music begins as I stand at the small barre in the back of the dressing room and go through a few quick exercises. I missed much of the group warm-up earlier due to my anxiety about checking the seats.

The fairies finish their dances and I hurry to the backstage area to join my minions. I'm about to go on.

There's really no way during this intense scene to easily look out, and the lights are so harsh, I couldn't make anything out anyway.

But as my pyrotechnics FLASH FLASH, I try to check the middle of the third row, where my family should be. I don't see a bunch of empty seats.

So maybe?

This energizes me, and I'm quite positive my

curse is the most vehement and diabolical of all the performances I've done, even for the DVD filming. I picture Andy clapping and laughing at his evil sister, and it's even more special.

Unlike many of the roles, Carabosse doesn't get an opportunity to bow after any of the dances, because the acting is too important. When I first saw the other characters do it, I asked Franco about it. He told me that virtually none of the modern ballets allowed Carabosse to bow, as it would take away from her evil character.

I wish I had one, though, so I could take a good hard look at the seats.

The ballet continues without issue through the prologue and all three acts. I text Blitz twice during intermissions, but I don't hear back. When we come out for our bows, I look out as best I can.

There is definitely not a group of empty seats, but I can't make out anything but movement in the glare of the lights shining directly at us. Sometimes the ushers fill in empty seats if audience members don't show up by intermission. I just don't know!

I race back to the dressing room to snatch up my phone. I swear I'm going to call Blitz myself when he finally writes me back. "I'm coming."

Who with?

He doesn't want to say. I don't know why.

I strip out of my costume as fast as possible and

put on my most demure outfit, a dark blue dress with a belted waist and miles of swinging skirt. A cashmere shrug covers my shoulders, and I look like something out of the fifties in it.

Dominika senses my stress and stands back to let the makeup artist remove the black blocks from my face. I tell her to keep my face plain and clean.

I take deep breaths as I head out into the hall. I see Blitz immediately in his funny hat. Then Mindy and her parents. And her little brother Owen, jostling with another boy.

Andy.

Oh my God.

It's Andy.

I let out a cry and run for him.

He sees me and heads my way, followed by the others.

I can't see anybody but him as I drop to my knees and envelop him in a hug. I'm crying, huge hot tears flowing down my face.

"Stop kissing me, Livia!" he says, wiping his cheeks. "You're supposed to be the bad guy!"

This makes everyone laugh.

I look up then, and my mother is there, looking uncertain in a long green dress. She seems older. It's been ten months since I have last spoken to her.

"Hello, Livia," she says.

I look behind her for my father, expecting his big frame and bigger scowl.

But he isn't there. Just Mindy's parents, looking pleased and proud. And Mindy, her hands clasped together, eyes shining.

I stand up. "You made it," I say.

She nods. "I only decided this morning." She glances around. "Your father wouldn't come. But I left anyway. I wanted to see."

Andy jumps up and down. "Where are the crows? I want to see them. Are there real people under there?"

"We can go see the costumes," I say to him.

Mindy comes forward to take his hand. "I'll take the boys there," she says. "Can Blitz show us the way?"

Blitz leads them down the hall. Mindy's parents murmur their congratulations on the show and move on.

And it's just me and my mom.

"You looked lovely up there," she says. "I was very proud."

I'm feeling everything at once. Happiness that she is here. Anger that my dad is not. So I can't help but say, "For a dirty whore?"

Mom's lips purse tightly. "He's a difficult man," she says. "I know it. I wonder sometimes if I should stay. But then where would he be without me? Where would I be without him?"

"I could buy you a house," I say. "Help you."

She nods. "I'm sure you could." She reaches out to touch my arm, her fingers trailing down the softness of the cashmere shrug. "You look so different. So sure of yourself. I'm glad."

I want to lash out, to tell her that it's despite them, not because of them. But she's here, and that's what I want. And my father is left out, alone back in San Antonio stewing in the anger that has poisoned him.

"I'm doing fine," I say. "I'm happy."

"I can see that." She looks behind her at the door to the dressing room where the others went. "I'd love to see the costumes too. And meet this man of yours."

So we go in where Andy and Owen are petting the feathers on the crow costumes. Two of the dancers are there, showing them how the beaks go on their heads.

Dominika is finishing with the makeup artist and looks regal in a royal blue evening gown. She nods at us as she passes, but I don't stop her for introductions. This is too hard already.

"Was that Aurora?" Mindy asks.

"Yes, she was a very famous ballerina in Russia," I say.

Everybody looks starstruck, as if Blitz isn't standing right behind us, ten thousand times more famous. But I get it. The ballet makes you feel this way, as if the dancers onstage made magic before your eyes.

Blitz steps forward then and puts his arm around me. "I met the lovely Wallers already," he says. "I assume this is your mother?"

I take in a deep breath. "Yes. Mom, this is Blitz. I still call him that, but his real name is Benjamin."

Mom extends her hand. "Hello, Benjamin. I'm Dorothy Mason."

Their shake is formal, but it's a start.

I glance up at Blitz. He's pleased with how everything is going, although I know he'll wonder why my father didn't come. Or maybe it's obvious. My father can't get past what's happened. Something in him just won't change, won't adjust, won't accept.

But as we move around the dressing room, then explore the other rooms and even sneak onto the stage, it's clear that whatever fear or anger or downright meanness has a hold on my dad, it is not part of my mother or my brother.

We all have a very late dinner together at a twenty-four-hour diner, squeezing into Blitz's limo while the boys start to crash. Ted stays out in the car with them asleep on the seats while we eat and Mom talks about Andy and church and the small events of their quiet life.

I hold Blitz's hand and feel wonder that I'm here. That they're here. That he's here. It's almost perfect. So close. My father doesn't matter.

But someone else does. And as I picture her, the way I last saw her, my heart crumbles a little on the edges.

I'll have to make do with what I've got.

Chapter Thirty-Two

The tour ends. Dmitri proclaims the entire season a smashing success and invites most of the cast to participate in casting for another ballet.

Andrew, Dominic, and Fiona sign up again. I haven't spoken to Carla since the flight to Houston, but I assume she will continue to pursue her dream.

The Prince is called to another company, leaving a prime spot open for a lead male dancer. I hope there is no rivalry that will drive a wedge between Andrew and Simon.

I decline to audition, unsure that another role will be quite as perfect for my immaturity in dance. And I'm also not certain that a life of endless ballet is really the best fit for me. Blitz will want to do projects too, and touring takes me away from him. It's my turn to follow him around.

When we touch down in San Antonio in Bennett's private plane, I can barely wait to get out and breathe the air of home again. It's October now, and Halloween is just around the corner. It will soon be exactly one year since I met Blitz.

I have Ted drive past Dreamcatcher on the way to our house. I've missed the sight of it. Seeing the big circular entrance and familiar parking lot fills me with nostalgia and hope.

"You should write Danika," Blitz says. "If Gabriella isn't doing lessons anymore, then we could go back."

He's right. As we head to our rented house, I craft a careful message. I've missed my lessons there, I say, and while I'm willing to stay away as long as necessary to protect Gabriella's privacy, if she isn't there, we'd love to return.

I don't get an answer right away and get caught up in unloading the car and walking around the house that I've missed so much since being on tour.

The pool sparkles in the back, and the living room smells of home. It's not very big, and the neighborhood has nothing special about it. But coming back to it makes me realize, I do love it.

When Ted has left, and I'm collapsed on the sofa, I ask Blitz, "So is this house only for rent? Is it not possible to buy it?"

The more I think about it, the more sense it

makes. It's close to Dreamcatcher. It's not far from Jenica's. There's no need to get something bigger or grander. We can live like normal people.

"I can check," Blitz says, picking up his phone to tap out a message. "Most people have a price."

I stare up at the ceiling. Even if we can't buy it, we can just stay here. It's fine. Pick a new project for Blitz. Maybe it will have something for me to do. Enjoy ourselves. Lie low. Avoid long commitments.

Blitz comes over to the sofa and lifts my legs to rest them on his lap. "This place was not the same without you," he says. "Not even close."

I watch him, the movement of the ceiling fan ruffling his dark hair. It's long again. I haven't been around to remind him to cut it, and he doesn't have Hannah or a stylist nagging him either. I like it. It's as if he's my Blitz now.

"I think San Antonio is a good base of operations," I say. "Maybe we can do *Dancing with the Stars* after all."

Blitz frowns. "Funny thing about that. Giselle made all that noise about getting me to come on, but neither of us are eligible to do it. We have non-compete clauses in our contracts that extend three years beyond the last episode we do of *Dance Blitz*."

This makes me laugh out loud. "She needs a new manager before she gets sued," I say.

"She needs to get a life." He runs his hands up and

down my legs. "It's about to be a year since we met," he says.

"I was just realizing that in the car. How should we celebrate?"

He tilts his head. "I might be able to cook something up."

"Just no live video feeds, okay?" I ask.

He laughs. "Those days are behind me. I swear."

"I'm still paranoid about cameras behind mirrors."

Blitz shifts until he's lying beside me, holding me against him so I don't fall off the cushions. "As long as I'm around, nobody will be spying on you but me."

"Oh, I don't know," I say. "We've taken the boy out of Hollywood, but I'm pretty sure there is still some Hollywood left in the boy."

He grins down at me. "Okay, I'm an attention whore. I admit it. But I'm seeing the value of downtime."

"How much longer?" I ask. "What do you already have planned?"

His smile is infectious. "Wouldn't you like to know?"

Chapter Thirty-Three

D anika texts the next day saying she'll get back to me about the academy. I take that to mean Gabriella is still there. Maybe she's trying to work out a deal where we go on different days.

I tell myself to be patient, but still find myself driving by to see if Gwen's SUV is there.

I meet Mom and Andy at the park. We swing and run around like the old days. Mom has promised my father not to bring me to his house, but he hasn't tried to ban her from seeing me. She has made it clear that if he tries it, she will leave.

I don't hold out hope for making up with him, but it's enough to see Mom and my brother. I haven't lost everything.

About a week after our return, Danika calls to say

she'd like for me and Blitz to come up to Dream-catcher to discuss options for classes.

It's an odd choice of day, a weekend afternoon, but I don't question it. I'm over the moon about the possibility of returning. We haven't worked out a single day since I've been back, not really wanting to go to Jenica's if we can get back where we want to go. Weeza is gone, though. Fiona texted me to say she was cast in a role in the next production, *A Midsummer Night's Dream*.

"Let's plan on doing some dancing while we're there," Blitz says, pulling his old jazz pants out of a drawer. "Something flashy."

I'm not sure about it, but since we're so close to our anniversary and back at Dreamcatcher at last, I pull out my blue leotards, his favorite, and a silky skirt.

When we get to the academy late that afternoon, the parking lot is jam-packed. We have to leave our car several blocks away.

"What is going on?" I ask as we walk up.

"Must be a busy part of the schedule," Blitz says.

He's jumpy, though, very un-Blitz-like.

"I don't buy it," I tell him. "You're up to something."

"It's just a little show," he says. "They might ask us to dance."

I stop in my tracks. "We haven't practiced

anything!" I say. "We haven't even danced together in months!"

He wraps an arm around my waist. "We could do something amazing in our sleep," he assures me. "And it's probably going to be nothing."

I let out a long sigh as we cross the parking lot and head up the stairs. I glance over at the wheelchair ramp. I don't even know if that class exists anymore. It may have never formed again after the break for summer.

I just have to be okay with that.

When we enter the foyer, Suze is at the desk. "Here's the program," she says. "Glad you guys could make it!"

"Thanks," Blitz says. He takes the folded page.

"Program for what?" I ask, snatching it from him. It's too early for the Christmas recital.

Danika is obviously doing something new. The academy is putting on a rendition of *Alice in Wonderland*. It includes ballet, tap, and contemporary numbers.

"I think it's about to start," Blitz says.

"We're going to watch it?"

"We are!" he says.

When we enter the crowded theater, it's hard to find seats. After months of front-row spots, it's amusing to have to ask someone to shift down a spot so we can have two together near the back. In the

DEANNA ROY

dim recital hall, nobody even notices who we are. The elderly couple sitting next to us clearly don't have a clue or don't care.

It's perfect.

We're barely settled when the lights go all the way down and the curtain opens slightly. Danika steps out and walks up to a lone microphone.

"I'm so glad you are all here," she says. "In the five years since Dreamcatcher Dance Academy opened, we have hosted ten recitals with individual numbers by our leveled classes." She pauses and smiles.

"This year, we decided to get a little more ambitious. Since classes began in August for the new term, we have had each group work on roles for a narrative work. We selected *Alice in Wonderland* because it has so many fun roles for children. The girl performing as Alice is one of our advanced dancers, and you will see all the children who take lessons here at Dreamcatcher throughout the performance. Thank you for coming."

The audience applauds. I'm thrilled to be here and see this, but it definitely isn't what I expected. I can't possibly take Danika aside for a meeting in the midst of all the activity.

Blitz takes my hand and I squeeze it. The curtain opens and Amanda, a girl from my advanced ballet class, comes out in a blue dress and apron. She must

266

be Alice. She wanders the stage alone, glancing around. The music begins, light and airy.

Five of Aurora's toddlers arrive, dressed as flowers. The audience collectively sighs and giggles as the little ones wiggle out onstage in green leotards and big petaled hats.

Aurora heads down to the floor and leads the girls in a little flower dance. Alice wanders among them, keeping them in line when needed. Then they toddle off.

A boy who is surely from Jacob's hip-hop class comes out, dressed as a white rabbit. The music shifts to an upbeat rhythm as he tries to convince Alice to come with him.

I glance over at Blitz. This is amazing.

Alice slides down the hole and goes through her process of eating and drinking to change size, along with dancers up on stilts, and then another round of teeny-tiny dancers for her to tower over.

Then the Mad Hatter arrives, and the back curtain goes up to reveal the tea party.

I almost jump out of my seat.

The wheelchair ballerinas are there, all of them! Gabriella!

I'm crying, just sobbing, to see her. They are all dressed in wild colors. The music is lively and quick. Then the girls all come around in front of the table to do a little dance with the teapots, passing them down and being silly as another older boy leaps around in his crazy tall hat.

There is much laughter in the room at their antics, but I can't stop crying. She's up there. She's right there!

Blitz videos it all with his phone while my attention is glued to the stage. The scene finishes and maybe it's just my imagination, but the applause is tremendous. I'm standing and cheering, then realize the show is moving on. I sit back down in embarrassment.

"You're fine," Blitz says. "You're not the only overzealous parent."

I wonder if Gwen saw me, if this is okay, or if she will be angry.

Then I realize — I was invited. Danika wanted me here. Even though Gabriella would be performing.

I settle back in my seat.

During the intermission, Blitz takes my hand. "We're wanted backstage."

My heart hammers. Will I get to see her?

"Is Gabriella there?" I ask.

"Not right away," he says. "But I believe we'll all be onstage together in the end."

"We will?"

We head to the front and zip up the stairs to the

stage, then duck between the side curtains to the backstage area.

Several parents dressed in black are rolling the tea-party table off the stage and pushing out a few fake trees.

I spot the Cheshire cat and Tweedledee and Tweedledum. They are definitely from Jacob's jazz class. Blitz gives each of them a high five. They are excited to see him.

We pass on through and into the storage area, where a huge path has been cleared to allow dancers to go to the opposite hall.

Then we're in the bright lights of the studios, kids everywhere. I peek into Studios 3 and 4, which are near the back, but the wheelchair ballerinas aren't in those.

"There's Danika," Blitz says, and pulls us into the Dance of the Shades room where we first met.

It's like coming home. The floor-to-ceiling images depict Juliet and her fellow ballerinas dancing the number the room is named for. I feel like I deserve to be here finally. My time doing *Sleeping Beauty* has given me that confidence.

"Oh, there you two are," Danika says. She passes a clipboard to Aurora, who is helping the toddlers put away their flower heads and find their mothers.

"We are ready and willing for duty," Blitz says.

Danika shakes her head with a laugh. "I forgot what a card you are. We're going to slide you in at the end of the party when Alice returns home. All the characters other than the toddlers will circle the stage."

"What are we going to do?" I shouldn't feel any panic about dancing after my stints on live TV, then having to prove myself before professional ballerinas, but I do.

"Whatever you like. Shall we play a waltz?" Danika asks.

"Way too slow," Blitz says. "Just give us a jazzy number and we'll roll with it."

"Sounds perfect," Danika says.

She's about to turn away when I say, "Wait!"

Danika's eyes meet mine. Her blue hair is recently re-dyed, vivid against her pale face. "You want to know about Gabriella," she says.

"Yes," I answer.

She glances at the other mothers and steps closer.

"Gwen has agreed to let you attend the recitals and say hello. Just not to teach her. No private lessons. And not to reveal your identity as her mother."

My throat goes tight. "Okay," I say.

"I assumed you would agree," she says. "She may come around yet. Let this be the start."

My eyes sting. "I will."

Blitz squeezes my hand. "You want to practice something or just wing it?" he asks.

"Are you crazy?" I ask him. "We're going to practice something."

As more of the sleepy toddlers file out, I pull him to the back corner of the room. "Show me what you've got, Blitz Craven."

"I thought you'd never ask."

Chapter Thirty-Four

I've been on a lot of stages.

There was the second season of *Dance Blitz*, the flat stage, when I stormed on unannounced.

There was the short third season. One prerecorded show and four live ones after they built that stage out to be larger and have two levels edged in neon.

I danced on eight different stages during our tour. Chicago, Boston, Baltimore, New York, Miami, Houston, LA, and Seattle. Some were bigger than others. Some fancier. Some historic. Some new.

But this stage is the one that matters.

I learned to dance on this stage.

I taught Blitz Craven, the most famous dancer in all of the country, to do a *grand jeté* on this stage.

I had my first recital here.

And today, I'm dancing with him in front of my daughter.

The kids form a circle around us, taking up the corners and leaving the center clear. It's less space than we're used to, but we can make do.

Because the fact is, together, Blitz and I can do anything.

We've come too far for me not to believe that.

The music begins, and the kids clap to the beat. We start strong as I run and leap into Blitz's arms and he launches me into the air.

I scissor above him and turn so that he can catch me. We're much braver now after doing aerial silks. This is nothing.

He slides me to the floor, and for a moment we tango, then move into a contemporary jitterbug. He spins me, I turn, then slide between his legs. I stop just inches from a ten-year-old boy from Jacob's class and kiss him on the cheek. He claps his hand to his face.

Then I'm back at Blitz. We're making it up as we go now, having only had time to work out the opening moves. But I know him. He knows me. We dance like other people have conversation.

The song is coming to a close, and I know he'll want to end dramatically. So I leap away from him to prepare for another pass at a lift.

He holds his hands and arms in a position I know.

It's how we communicate, in gestures and angles. I run toward him and jump as I get near. He grabs my feet and launches me up again. This time I turn and come down horizontally. He catches me and dips me, head near the floor. As the music ends with three pounding notes, we hold our position.

The kids jump to their feet.

By the time he sets me down, we're surrounded, children holding on to my legs, hanging on to Blitz. Danika comes out, but instead of speaking into the microphone she holds, she passes it to Blitz.

The kids don't leave us, but sit right where we stand.

Blitz takes my hand.

"Livia Mason," he says, his breathing still rapid, and maybe with a small waver in it. I immediately clasp his fingers harder, wondering what has gotten him shaken up. "We met right here at Dreamcatcher Dance Academy!"

There are cheers then, led by the other dance teachers, and the kids quickly follow their lead. We have to wait a moment for it to die down.

"It's been an entire year now, and I think everybody in the world has wondered why I've waited so long."

He drops to one knee.

Now I get it. His nervousness. The dance. The kids all around us.

I look at him, his hair sticking to his forehead, the blue of his shirt making his eyes stand out, his black hair gleaming. My Blitz. My Benjamin. My love.

"I know a famous ballerina like yourself may not find an out-of-work dancer like me a great catch," he says. The audience laughs.

"But if you'll have me, it would be the greatest honor of my life if you would be my wife." He swallows hard, his Adam's apple bobbing before he goes on. "Will you marry me?"

One of the boys near him nudges him and says, "You better have a ring." There is more laughter.

Blitz fumbles with the microphone and reaches in his pocket. A ring box wouldn't fit in those pants, no way, but it's just the ring. A diamond, princess cut of course, the rectangle as wide as my finger and surrounded by blue gems the exact color of that first leotard I wore just for him. Like today.

I try to answer and find my voice isn't quite working, so I just nod for yes.

The cheers are tremendous and it feels like the roof will lift right off. Blitz slides the ring on my finger and stands up to take me in his arms.

His kiss is warm and tender and full of promise. To have and to hold. Till death do us part. I can feel the words as if he's saying them.

When he finally lets us go, I find the wheelchair ballerinas have pushed their way to the center. We hug each of them. When I get to Gabriella, I keep my embrace as close to the others as I can, but I breathe her in, the strawberry shampoo, the hair spray, the little girl I remember.

When I look out in the audience, I spot my brother running forward. My mom holds out her arm, unable to stop him. I catch her eyes and she shrugs. She wipes the corner of her eye.

Then he's up with us, my baby brother, Andy, and we're hugging. The teachers walk up to lead the children off the stage. Danika takes the microphone to thank everyone for coming.

It's all a fog, the sound, the lights, the movement.

Gwen comes onstage to get Gabriella and our gazes meet for just a moment. She keeps a tight smile as she pushes Gabriella away.

I got to see her. I will see her. She isn't lost.

My mom comes up and watches me gaze after them.

"That's her, isn't it?" she asks.

I nod.

"She looks exactly like you," Mom says.

"Who does? Who does?" Andy asks.

"Just one of the dancers," I say. "She has the same color hair as me."

Andy is not impressed by this and takes my hand. "Can we go get ice cream?" he asks. "Can I have sprinkles?"

Blitz ruffles his hair. "As long as Mom says it's all right, that sounds like a perfect plan."

I glance out at the rapidly emptying recital hall. For a moment I catch a glimpse of a man by the door and swear it is my father.

But then he's gone, and Blitz is leading the four of us down the stairs to the seats. I don't even know if it was him.

"How did you know to come?" I ask Mom.

"Benjamin called," she says. She tugs a phone out of her bag, a new one. "He gave me our own special way to communicate back in Houston." She sticks it back in her bag. "Your dad knows about it."

I shove my shoulder against Blitz's. "You and your surprise phones."

"It's my only party trick," he says.

Before we pass through the exit doors, I turn back to look at the empty stage. The lights are still up, and the velvet curtains are open, stirring slightly in the current of air from the vents.

I never imagined this would be my life. That it would start someplace like this.

But Dreamcatcher has been the place where I discovered who I could be, that best self that was waiting for one thing. For me to believe in her.

Mom and Andy have walked ahead, but Blitz waits for me, looking where I look. If anyone understands, it's him. He drapes his arm across my shoulders.

"Good things happen here," he says.

I lean in close, my head resting on his shoulder. The light sparkles through the new ring on my finger.

"The best things happen here," I say.

And I believe they have only just begun.

I hope you enjoyed *Tender Dance*! In the final book of the series, Blitz and Livia plan their quiet wedding. But guess who has other plans? See the fight between Hollywood and our couple for the biggest wedding in television history as the *Lovers Dance* series comes to a close in Final Dance.

Also by Deanna Roy

The Forever Series

A young couple reunites in colleges, four years after the death of their newborn.

Book one Forever Innocent *is FREE on all venues.*

- Forever Innocent (Corabelle & Gavin)
- Forever Loved (Corabelle & Gavin)
- Forever Sheltered (Tina & Darion)
- Forever Bound (Jenny & Chance)
- Forever Family (Corabelle, Tina, Jenny)
- Forever Christmas (Corabelle & Gavin)

- Boxed Set: First Three Books
- Boxed Set: Final Three Books

- Stella and Dane (Standalone)

The Lovers Dance Series

A sheltered ballerina is lured into the life of a brash TV reality show star.

- Forbidden Dance
- Wounded Dance
- Wicked Dance
- Tender Dance
- Final Dance

- Lovers Dance Boxed Set

- Billionaire's Dance (a standalone prequel)

Other Books

- Conversations with Little Dude (Nonfiction stories with her son who was adopted from foster care)
- In the Company of Angels (A fill-in-the-pages baby record book for babies lost to miscarriage or stillbirth)
- The Magic Mayhem trilogy of action/adventure books for children ages 9-12.

If you prefer your romances with no graphic love scenes or coarse language

You will love Deanna's pen name Abby Tyler. As Abby, Deanna writes funny, feel-good small-town romances with

a recurring cast of feisty senior citizens and the couples they push together, by hook or by crook.

Deanna is the six-time *USA Today* bestselling author of romance and women's fiction.

She is a passionate advocate for women who have miscarried. She founded the web site Pregnancy-Loss.info in 1998 after the loss of her first baby and continues to run both online and in-person support groups for women who have endured this impossible loss.

She is a foster mom, an adoptive mom, and a baby loss mom. She lives in Austin, Texas, with her family.

Learn more about the author at
www.deannaroy.com

Join her email or text list for new release notices at
Deanna's List

facebook.com/deannaroyauthor

twitter.com/deannaroy

instagram.com/deannaroyauthor

goodreads.com/Goodreads

bookbub.com/authors/deanna-roy

Sneak Peek of Final Dance

I whirl around. It's Hannah, Blitz's agent. She's standing down the hall all stark and skinny, like a coat rack.

I tense up. We haven't spoken to Hannah since she orchestrated a comeback for the three jilted finalists, the ones who lost their chance with Blitz when I stormed onto the finale of the show and claimed him for myself.

Blitz was justifiably angry that his agent involved them, sparking a lawsuit that caused us to do a shortened season three of the show.

I still won.

But I lost a lot in the process. My anonymity. My privacy.

And, almost, access to the little girl I gave up for adoption when I was fifteen.

"Where is wardrobe?" I ask the short woman. I don't want to talk to Hannah, especially without Blitz. She isn't my agent. I have no business with her.

And I hold grudges too.

The girl recognizes a fight, though, and doesn't move.

Hannah approaches, her heels ringing on the shiny floor. She's as stilted and perfect as always in an immaculate lime green pencil skirt and matching jacket. Her blond hair sweeps her face in a smooth bob.

"Livia," she says, "why don't we put that ring someplace safe until it's time for Blitz to give it to you on the air?" She reaches out a hand.

I turn away from her. "No."

"Be reasonable. Blitz's contract specifically states that in the event of an engagement to one of the finalists of the show, the proposal is the property of the franchise and will be aired exclusively by the network."

"It's my engagement," I say.

"You're under contract too," she says coldly.

I look at her then. "You don't manage me."

Hannah sighs. "I'll send someone to reason with

you." She waves her hands airily. "But I wouldn't let anyone see it. I would hate for a breach of contract lawsuit to wipe out your earnings from the show." She starts walking down the hall, the sharp tap of her shoes starting up again.

I clasp my hand around the ring. "We already got engaged," I call after her. "You can't erase that it already happened."

Hannah laughs but doesn't turn around as she calls out, "If his millions of fans didn't see it, then it *didn't happen*."

She turns the corner and disappears.

See the fight between Hollywood and our couple for the biggest wedding in television history as the *Lovers Dance* series comes to a close in Final Dance.

www.ingramcontent.com/pod-product-compliance
Lightning Source LLC
Chambersburg PA
CBHW070922260626
47162CB00007B/2761